PLEASE DON'T FEED THE MAYOR

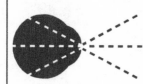

This Large Print Book carries the
Seal of Approval of N.A.V.H.

PLEASE DON'T FEED THE MAYOR

SUE PETHICK

THORNDIKE PRESS

A part of Gale, a Cengage Company

Farmington Hills, Mich • San Francisco • New York • Waterville, Maine
Meriden, Conn • Mason, Ohio • Chicago

LIBRARY OF CONGRESS CIP DATA ON FILE.
CATALOGUING IN PUBLICATION FOR THIS BOOK
IS AVAILABLE FROM THE LIBRARY OF CONGRESS

ISBN-13: 978-1-4328-6419-4 (hardcover alk. paper)

Published in 2019 by arrangement with Kensington Books, an imprint of Kensington Publishing Corp.

Printed in Mexico
1 2 3 4 5 6 7 23 22 21 20 19

To Chris, with gratitude and love

Chapter 1

Melanie MacDonald woke that morning with a start. Maybe it was a bad dream that had caused it or just the mysterious workings of her subconscious, but the second she opened her eyes a terrible certainty clutched at her heart: Fossett — the town she loved best in all the world — was dying. Blinking back tears, her heart pounding, she groped toward the foot of the bed where her border collie, Shep, was sleeping. As he lifted his head and nuzzled her hand, Melanie took a deep breath and felt the constriction in her chest begin to ease.

"We can't let it happen, boy," she whispered. "We've got to find a way to save this place."

A glance at the clock told her she'd beaten the alarm by twenty minutes — something Melanie would ordinarily have spent on some extra shut-eye — but sleep would be impossible now. Better to get up than to lie there in the darkness and fret, she thought. Plus, it would give her time to think before she headed in to work. There was still time to save her little town, she told herself. The only question was: How?

The brisk October air made her face tingle as she opened the back door for Shep. It was her favorite time of year, a period of growing anticipation between the enervating heat of summer and the first snowfall. Songbirds were emptying her feeders as fast as she could fill them, and in spite of Shep's best efforts the squirrels had already buried an orchard's worth of nuts in her backyard. Down in the river, the last of the late-season Chinook were racing upstream, and the pumpkins she'd planted in July would be jack-o'-lanterns before long. If only other people could see the town the way she did, Melanie thought as she headed back inside, Fossett's problems would be over.

Shep continued to romp in the backyard while Melanie made breakfast. She stood at the kitchen window, watching him zigzag across the lawn, guiding his soccer ball around a stile and into an upturned orange crate. The border collie's previous owners had given him away when he refused to stop herding their small children around like sheep, and she'd made it a priority to channel those instincts toward something less objectionable. Much as she enjoyed having him with her at work, Melanie knew that being inside all day was hard on a working dog and letting him tire himself out a bit first made life at the coffee shop easier for everyone.

When her toast came up, Melanie sat down at the table and began racking her brain once again for ways to save Fossett from extinction. The town's troubles weren't news to anyone; its residents had already spent time and money trying to improve its fading prospects. The old Fossett House, a Victorian mansion built for a railroad baron's mistress, had been remodeled into a bed-and-breakfast, money had been raised to modernize the school, and Main Street had undergone a complete overhaul with fountains, bubblers, and wrought iron benches for people to enjoy during their shopping trips. But in spite of those improvements, folks were still moving away and the future seemed bleaker than ever. If something drastic wasn't done, Fossett would soon be nothing but a historical footnote.

She hung her head and fought the urge to cry. Had moving back there been a mistake? It was so easy at times like that to start second-guessing herself. It wasn't just that she'd sunk her life savings into the coffee shop; she'd given up everything else, too: friends, a good job, even her marriage had fallen to the wayside. Melanie had bet her entire future on making things work in her hometown. If they didn't, it wouldn't just mean that her business had failed; it would also mean she'd sacrificed everything for a foolish dream. She didn't think she could face that.

Melanie looked up and frowned; Shep was pawing anxiously at the front door. He must have let himself in while she was brooding, she thought, but what on earth was he so worked up about? Then she glanced at her watch.

"Oh, my gosh, look at the time!"

She grabbed her coat and the two of them ran out the door.

Ground Central was in the heart of Fossett's downtown, one of a dwindling number of shops still thriving on Main Street. Even as other businesses closed, Melanie had managed to hang on, a fact she attributed to Shep. As the shop's official greeter, he made everyone who walked through the door feel welcome.

Melanie turned on the television and

started filling the two large coffee urns while Shep walked through the dining area, nudging chairs into place around the tables. The constant drone of entertainment news hadn't been part of her original plan when she opened Ground Central — she'd been picturing more of a quiet coffee bar like the ones they had in Portland and Seattle — but resistance on the part of Fossett's populace and the need to meet her financial obligations had convinced her that compromise was necessary to her survival. As frustrating as it felt sometimes, she could at least console herself that Ground Central had achieved its main purpose: to become an informal neighborhood gathering place.

The smell of coffee brewing filled the air as Melanie made a last pass through the shop, refilling stir sticks and sweetener packets while Shep waited patiently for Walt Gunderson to arrive. Walt was the owner of Gunderson's, the grocery/hardware/feed store that had been the heart and soul of Fossett for five generations, and his wife, Mae, made the baked goods that Melanie sold in her shop. Walt had been both mentor and father figure to her the last four years, and as owner of one of the few thriving businesses in town, he was as keen to find a way of improving Fossett's prospects as she was. He was also, as Shep knew, a soft touch when it came to giving out his wife's homemade dog treats.

When Walt's truck arrived, Shep's ears pricked up. Licking his chops in anticipation, he trotted toward the front door to greet his benefactor and, with his head lowered obligingly and his bottom wiggling, Shep stretched his upper lip into an unmistakable doggie grin. Melanie scolded him as she hurried over to unlock the door.

"Shep," she said. "Don't be a beggar."

"It's fine," Walt said, holding the box aloft. "Hold on, boy. Let me put these down and we'll see what Mae's sent for you today."

He set the box on the counter and reached into his pocket as Shep swallowed dramatically.

"Well, well. What's this?" Walt said, holding the bone-shaped biscuit to his nose. "Smells like peanut butter."

Shep whimpered and squirmed impatiently.

"Oh, all right. Here you go."

He tossed the treat into the air.

Shep leaped, grabbed the proffered treat in his mouth, and hurried over to his bed in the corner to enjoy it in peace.

Walt laughed. "I think that's the highest I've ever seen him jump. Mae will be pleased."

Melanie poured Walt the cup of coffee he took in exchange for a discount on the baked goods and pushed it across the counter.

"So," she said, indicating the box on the counter, "what have you brought *me* today?"

"Blueberry muffins and oatmeal scones."

She lifted the lid and felt her mouth form an o in surprise.

"What are those?"

"Selma's latest creation. She asked me to include them in this week's deliveries."

Selma Haas was the manager of the newly renovated Fossett House B and B. With business slower than expected, she spent her time thinking up ways to enhance the enjoyment of her imaginary guests.

"She calls 'em Beavertails."

Melanie poked one with her finger. "But what *are* they?"

"Brownies. She told Mae she cooks 'em in a muffin pan and then flattens 'em with a spatula while they're still warm." Walt pointed. "That's what gives them their crisscross pattern."

"And . . . they're supposed to look like a beaver's tail?"

"Something like. She thinks they'll give

13

the tourists 'an authentic Northwest experience.' "

"Assuming we ever *get* any tourists around here."

Walt nodded. "The woman's got an imagination; I'll give her that."

A slow smile spread across Melanie's face. "Maybe we should call them Eaverbay Eeltays."

The two of them shared a guilty chuckle. Selma had been hired as manager of the B and B on the strength of her claim that she was bilingual. It was only later that anyone discovered the "foreign language" she spoke was pig Latin.

The moment of levity passed, leaving Melanie as dispirited as she'd been when she woke up that morning. She sighed and slumped against the counter.

"Oh, Walt, what are we going to do? I've been cogitating till my brains are scrambled, trying to figure out how to save this place."

He shook his head. "I'm not sure there's anything we can do. At the moment, my plan is to wait till Social Security kicks in, then close up shop and move to someplace warmer."

"You can't mean that."

"Why not? This place has broken my heart too many times, Mel. There comes a time

14

when a man has to admit defeat."

She shook her head, unwilling to adopt his pessimistic attitude. There had to be a way, Melanie thought. She just hadn't found it yet.

Walt reached across the counter and patted her arm.

"I know how you feel, but at this point, I'm not really sure this place is salvageable. Look at the folks we've lost: professionals, small-business owners, families with children — the people a town needs to build a foundation on." He looked askance at the Beavertails. "Aside from the two of us and the guy who owns the bar, the most successful people in town are a pet psychic and the gals with the pot farm."

Melanie held up a hand in protest.

"Okay, first of all, it's not a pot farm; they grow *medicinal* marijuana."

Walt rolled his eyes as she continued.

"And sure, Fossett's got its fair share of oddballs — maybe even more than its fair share — but that's just local color. People like Jewell Divine add a dash of whimsy that's charming," she said. "We just need to find a way to attract some normal people to Fossett, to sort of . . . dilute the ones that are already here."

Walt wasn't buying it.

"People don't want to live around a bunch of weirdos," he said. "I'm sorry, but short of a miracle, I don't think Fossett's got a chance in hell."

The morning breakfast crowd started arriving as soon as Walt drove away, and it was almost ten o'clock before the place emptied out again. Someone had cranked up the volume on the TV set and with no human voices to cover the sound, the reporter's voice was giving her a headache. She grabbed the remote and was about to turn it down when she saw the headline at the bottom of the screen:

English Town Elects Cat to Local Council

"This is Chad Chapman, reporting to you from the tiny English village of Croton-by-the-Sea, where its single seat on the county council has been given to Reginald, a ten-year-old tabby cat belonging to Miss Pansy Suggitt."

The camera angle widened to show an orange-and-white tabby, lying on a pillow in what appeared to be a tobacconist's shop. A man with a microphone stood next to him, facing the camera.

"Since his election, 'Reggie' has become

something of a celebrity in his little town. Dozens of tourists arrive by bus each day, hoping to meet the new 'councilfeline.' "

Dozens every day? Melanie thought. A shiver of excitement passed through her.

"Cards and letters addressed to 'Councilman Reggie' quickly overwhelmed the local postal authorities, who have had to bring in extra help to handle the overload, but few people are complaining, as sales of merchandise with the tabby's likeness have boosted the local economy and put this sleepy little hamlet on the map."

Melanie's heart was racing. This was exactly the sort of thing that Fossett needed: a bold move that would get people excited again. They might not have a town council, but they could figure something out. All they really needed was the right animal to fill the position. And that, she thought, glancing over at Shep, would be easy.

CHAPTER 2

Melanie's hands shook as she set out the last of the folding chairs. In the three days since she'd come up with her plan, she'd lost two pounds and chewed off all but one of her fingernails. If this town hall meeting didn't go well, she feared she'd never come up with another idea as promising. There'd be no other option then but to watch Fossett continue its downhill slide.

A bead of sweat snaked its way down her temple. Melanie wiped it away as she counted the number of seats crowding the floor of her coffee shop. How many people would show up? she wondered. Folks in Fossett weren't particularly "churchy," but most still thought of Sundays as sacred, even if all it meant was getting an extra hour or two of sleep. She'd posted flyers on every street corner and several people had told her they'd be there, but saying and doing were two very different things. What she needed was a representative sample of residents to test her idea on, but with five minutes to go and no one in sight, she feared even that modest goal had been too ambitious.

If only she'd been able to convince Walt.

In spite of his admission that her plan had merit, Walt Gunderson remained stubbornly convinced that any idea — even one as unconventional as making Shep the mayor — was doomed to failure. The last time they'd spoken, he advised her not to look for him at the meeting. As Melanie grabbed another chair and set it in place, she tried to ignore the knot in her stomach.

"Where do you want these cookies?" Kayla said.

Melanie looked up at the girl in the heavy metal T-shirt. For the first few years after opening Ground Central, Melanie had labored alone, unable to afford even part-time help. Then five months ago, she'd finally hired her first permanent employee. Kayla Maas might be only eighteen and her fashion choices somewhat questionable, but she showed up on time, didn't cop an attitude with the customers, and adored Shep, for whom the feeling was mutual.

"The front counter is fine," Melanie said. "Are the coffee urns ready?"

"Yep. Regular on the right, Unleaded on the left." Kayla set the tray down and covered it with plastic wrap. "How many people will come, you think?"

"Who knows? Twenty? Thirty? None?"

There was a handprint on the front door. Melanie walked into the back room to get some vinegar water and a rag.

"You think Mr. Gunderson will change his mind?" Kayla said.

She shook her head.

"I doubt it."

"I don't get it," the girl said, dusting crumbs off the counter. "That story about the cat said it brought a lot of people into the town. If it worked there, why not here?"

"It's not that he thinks having Shep as the mayor won't work," Melanie said. "It's just that, well, he's not sure that anything will help save Fossett at this point."

"Why not?"

She bit her lip, wondering how to paraphrase Walt's position without giving offense. After all, it wasn't as if his objections were unfounded.

"Because we don't just need people to come and visit; we need for them to move here permanently. I think he's afraid that most folks won't find Fossett all that appealing."

Kayla scrunched up her nose.

"What's wrong with it?"

"Oh, you know. It's a small town. People in small towns can be a bit . . . different." She chuckled. "I mean, it's not every place that has a pet psychic."

"But people love Jewell!" Kayla said. "And she's really good, too. When our cockatiel, Stevie, stopped eating, Mom asked Jewell to come over and take a look at him. Right away, she knew what was wrong."

Melanie nodded feebly. She could just picture Jewell Divine, showing up on Kayla's doorstep in one of her tie-dyed caftans, ready to reveal the thoughts and feelings of the anorexic bird.

"Jewell told us that Stevie had been smuggled in from South America in some guy's smelly coat and then sold to a pet store where the other birds were mean to him. It was real sad."

"And did he start eating again?"

"Oh no, he died," Kayla said. "But at least we understood him better, and Jewell said sometimes that's all an animal really wants. Plus, after all he'd been through, we could sort of understand why he'd want to end it all."

"So . . . it was suicide?"

"Yeah, I guess so."

Melanie was about to say something about the chances that a bird would willfully self-destruct when the girl's phone rang. As Kayla went off to answer it, Melanie started cleaning the window, going over what she planned to say at the meeting as she wiped away the handprints. Now wasn't the time to worry about whether or not Walt was right, she told herself. Making Shep the mayor was going to be enough of a stretch without complicating matters, and it was important that the idea get more than a grudging endorsement. For her plan to work, Fossett's residents would need to know they had a stake in the outcome. The last thing she wanted was for anyone to feel they'd been buffaloed.

Kayla returned and glanced at the door.

"I'm surprised there's nobody here yet."

Melanie felt the knot in her stomach tighten.

"Yeah. I guess free coffee and cookies weren't as enticing as I thought."

"Mind if I take off, then? I told Cal I'd go kayaking with him today."

"No, you go on," Melanie said. "I appreciate your helping out. See you tomorrow."

As Kayla disappeared around the corner, Melanie sauntered up to the front counter, lifted the plastic wrap from the cookies, and slid one off the tray. To help keep her strength up when everyone arrived, she told herself, taking a bite. Or as consolation, if no one did.

Then, like the first drops of rain after a long drought, people began to arrive. A trickle at first, then groups of two and three came in, chatting amiably as they surveyed the cookies, poured themselves some coffee, and found a seat. Selma from the B and B came, taking an extra cookie for the boy who was watching the front desk, along with her twin sister, Helena, and Jewell Divine, in a pair of harem pants and a tie-dyed vest. Rod Blakely arrived in his usual attire — jungle fatigues, combat boots, and a flak jacket — and Francine and Everett Stubbs had left their herd of goats to take their places in the front row. When the flow of friends and neighbors finally abated, fifty-one people — more than twice as many as expected — had shown up. Melanie searched the faces carefully, but Walt's was not among them. She told herself it shouldn't have been a surprise. Nevertheless, his lack of confidence felt like a blow.

She stepped up in front of the counter and cleared her throat.

"Thanks for coming, everyone," she said, loud enough to be heard over the din.

As the room quieted, all eyes turned toward her. Seeing so many hopeful faces made Melanie feel weak at the knees. These were her friends and neighbors, people hoping for a way out of a desperate situation, and what did she have to offer them? An absurd idea based on something that had happened half a world away. What if Walt was right and Fossett was already beyond salvation? All she'd be giving them was another dose of false hope. Melanie looked down at her ragged fingernails and felt the weight of their expectations pressing down on her. Perhaps, she thought, it would be better just to admit defeat and go home.

A whoosh of air and the sound of chairs being shuffled caught her attention. She looked up and saw the door close as Walt Gunderson slipped inside. He leaned against the back wall, arms folded, and gave her an encouraging nod. Melanie felt tears of relief and gratitude well up. Maybe this wasn't a lost cause after all.

"We all know that things around here have been going downhill since the mill closed. Shops are closing, people are moving away, and the changes we thought would bring more people into town haven't worked out the way we hoped."

Heads nodded. There were murmurs of assent.

"I have an idea that I think might help, something that would get us some attention and bring tourists into town."

"We don't need tourists," Rod Blakely grumbled. "We need jobs."

"You're right," Melanie said. "We do need jobs, but we need people, too. Folks who have jobs in Corvallis or Albany — even Salem — might just be looking for a small town where they can raise their kids. If we can get the word out about what a great place Fossett is, I think folks like that will want to come here and buy houses, settle down, and fill our school with their kids so we can reverse the downward spiral we've been in."

"The mill's closed," someone said. "Those jobs aren't coming back."

"No," she said. "But if we can increase our numbers, Fossett will be a more attractive place for companies to come to. We've got a lot of empty storefronts to fill."

"Retail jobs don't pay enough to live on," said another.

"Yeah," Rod Blakely added. "Minimum wage won't help anyone."

Melanie was tempted to point out that rents were dirt cheap in Fossett and having any job was better than being unemployed, but she didn't want to get pulled into an argument before she'd had a chance to share her idea. Making Shep the mayor was never going be the entire solution to Fossett's problems, but it could be a step toward helping the town rehabilitate itself. If they got bogged down in the details now, people might give up before they'd even given it a chance.

"So," came a voice from the back. "What's your idea?"

Melanie gave Walt a grateful smile. He might be a skeptic, but he'd come and shown his support. Whether or not he'd ever change his mind, it seemed he at least wanted people to hear what she had to say.

"I think we need a gimmick," she said.

At once, the air of excited anticipation died. Heads shook and eyes began to roll. Melanie felt panic rise up in her chest. How could they dismiss her so quickly? They hadn't even heard what she had to say. She gave Walt a pleading look, hoping for some backup.

"Quiet down!" he said. "You all sound like a bunch of geese. Let the lady finish."

The effect was immediate. Against the moral weight of their most prominent citizen no one was willing to argue.

"So, what's the gimmick?" Selma said.

Melanie paused. Thinking about making her dog the mayor was one thing, but saying it out loud almost made it seem like a joke. She didn't want people to think she was making fun of their plight or minimizing the amount of effort it would take to drag them back from the brink of disaster. What made her think that her plan would work when so many others had failed?

Then Melanie glanced at Shep, sitting beside her, alert but unruffled by a crowd whose emotions were wavering between hope and despair, and it occurred to her that he was exactly the sort of leader they needed. Maybe having Shep as Fossett's mayor wasn't so crazy after all, she told herself. Maybe, under the circumstances, it was the sanest thing they could do. She just had to hope that the people who saw him sitting there would realize it, too.

"I think we need a mayor."

"A *mayor*?!"

"Oh, come on."

"What the hell kind of gimmick is that?"

"Hold on!" Walt said. "Let her finish."

"And," Melanie added, "I think it should be my dog, Shep."

For the first few seconds, no one moved. The coffee shop was so quiet she could hear the clock ticking on the wall behind her. Melanie swallowed, and the sound seemed to fill the room as she waited for a response.

I am never going to live this down.

Then everyone began to talk at once.

"That's a great idea!"

"A dog mayor! We'll be famous!"

"It's perfect!"

"Three cheers for Mayor Shep!"

As the crowd continued to smile and voice their approval, Melanie glanced at Walt, who shook his head in wonder. The folks there had not only taken her seriously; they also seemed to think her plan could work. It wasn't the end of Fossett's problems by a long shot, but it was a start.

And it was already catching fire.

"He should wear a badge that says: 'Mayor Shep.' "

"And carry a briefcase!"

"Why don't we give him an office in the old City Hall building?"

"Yeah, people could come and see him passing laws."

"Mayors don't pass laws; they enforce them."

"No, the police do that!"

"Well, Fossett doesn't *have* a police force, does it?"

"Good thing, too, or you'd be in jail!"

"Wait!" Melanie shouted, waving her arms. "Hold on! Shep wouldn't be doing things that a real mayor would do. He'd just be the *honorary* mayor."

Disappointed looks were exchanged among the audience members.

"What's the point of that?"

"The point is, he'd be *called* the mayor and people would come and see him."

"But if he's not a real mayor —"

"He would be a real mayor," Melanie said. "A real, *honorary* mayor. Cities do it all the time."

Nevertheless, the air of skepticism remained.

"But what would he *do*?"

"The same thing he does now: greet people at the coffee shop and nap on his dog bed."

"Who'd want to come all the way out here just to see that?"

"Lots of people," Melanie said, her confidence waning. "He's a dog. People love dogs."

Now that they were talking about the actual details of her plan, she had to admit that the idea sounded awfully flimsy. The story on the television hadn't said anything about Reginald the cat doing anything special, but that was in England. Maybe

Americans needed something more exciting to get them to come to a place like Fossett.

"I don't know," Selma said. "I still think he needs to do some mayor stuff."

"Well . . . maybe he could be a real mayor," Melanie conceded. "But before we decide about that, we need to agree that this is something we all want to do. If people here in town don't take this seriously, no one else will believe it and the whole thing will fall apart. What we have to decide today is, should we do it or not?"

"You can't decide something like that on the say-so of a couple dozen people," Rod Blakely said. "That ain't fair."

Melanie ground her teeth. Leave it to Rod, she thought, to stop her momentum in its tracks.

"All right," she said. "What would you suggest?"

"We should put it to a vote."

"Right now?" She looked around.

"No. On Election Day."

"But that's silly. He'd be the only candidate."

"Not necessarily." Rod gave her a mutinous look. "There might be others who'd like to be the mayor."

She should have seen this coming, Melanie thought. Rod Blakely was not only the most disagreeable person in Fossett; he was also under the impression that he was the smartest, most competent, and best-loved guy in town. The man was delusional.

"Look, I really don't see why we should hold an election. After all, the point is to have a *dog* as our mayor."

Rod crossed his arms. "No, the point is to make the process *fair.*"

Melanie was dismayed to find several people nodding in agreement. Folks in Fossett might not be terribly sophisticated, but they had a keen sense of right and wrong; fairness and playing by the rules meant more to them than reason and logic. She glanced at Walt, hoping for some sort of intervention, but he simply shrugged as if to say, *You got yourself into this mess. Better figure your way out.*

"All right," she said. "We'll hold an election."

"On Election Day?" Selma said.

"Uh, sure, I guess. If we can manage it."

"But we don't have a mayor *now.* How do we elect one?"

Melanie shook her head, feeling the optimism that had carried her thus far begin to falter under the weight of reality.

"I-I suppose the first thing we'll have to do is talk to an attorney and find out what the legal requirements are."

Francine Stubbs scowled.

"And how much will *that* cost?"

"Yeah," her husband said. "I thought this was supposed to *make* us money, not *cost* us anything."

As the rumbles of dissent grew, Melanie knew she'd have to act fast.

"It's all right," she said. "I know a lawyer who'll do it for *free.*"

And just like that, the tide turned back in her favor. Hopeful smiles broke out all over the room and people came forward to shake Shep's paw, promising him their votes. Walt Gunderson gave her a thumbs-up and she nodded her thanks. She'd done it! And once the people there went back to their homes and families, the idea would percolate and grow until everyone in Fossett would be eager to have Shep as their mayor.

Sure, they'd have to hold an election and Rod Blakely might insist that his name be on the ballot, but no one in their right mind would vote for him, so why worry? All she needed to do was figure out how to hold an election that was legally enforceable in the next two weeks. Never mind that the only lawyer Melanie knew was her ex-husband, or that she hadn't spoken to him in years, or even that they'd broken up over his refusal to move to Fossett. That was history, over and done with. The two of them had moved on ages ago. He'd be happy to help her out, right?

CHAPTER 3

Bryce MacDonald could be forgiven for feeling a bit smug. Not only had he just won a big case, but billable hours for his first year at Norcross Daniels had exceeded all expectations; if things continued as they were, he'd be pocketing a hefty bonus at the end of the year. As he prepared for his defense team's debrief with the senior partner that afternoon, he finally felt as if his decision to become a litigator had been the right one. It was hard to imagine that sixteen months ago he'd been busting his butt in the DA's office and drowning in student debt. Whoever said that money couldn't buy a clear conscience didn't know what they were talking about.

The intercom buzzed.

"Call for you on line three. It's Melanie Mac-Donald."

Seconds passed while Bryce hesitated. He glanced at his watch. The debrief was in eighteen minutes.

"Did she say what it was regarding?"

"No, sir."

Bryce considered the possibilities. Was it an emergency of some sort? The last time they'd spoken, she made it clear that she didn't need his help. A death in the family? Doubtful. Melanie was an only child of only children, a late-in-life baby whose parents had died when she was barely out of her teens.

He pressed his lips together, feeling an unreasonable irritation at this intrusion. Why was she calling now, just when things were looking up for him? The blinking light on his telephone seemed as ominous as a ticking time bomb.

"Shall I ask her to leave a message?"

"No." He shook his head. "No, it's fine. I'll take it."

He took a deep breath and put it on speakerphone, hoping to get whatever had prompted this call over and done with quickly. It was like tearing off a bandage, he told himself. The faster you did it, the sooner the pain went away.

"MacDonald here."

"Hey, it's me. Been a long time, huh?"

Hearing her voice again was like a physical blow. It *had* been a long time, he thought. A long time and no time at all. Bryce swallowed.

"Hi, Mel. What's up?"

"I've got a legal problem I could really use your help with."

"What sort of legal problem?"

She laughed. "Don't worry, I'm not in jail or anything."

Bryce's heart was pounding.

"Go on."

"The thing is, I need to know how to hold an election — a legal one — in Oregon."

So, this wasn't a personal call, he thought, just business. That was good. Bryce had spent years learning how to separate his emotions from the law. He started gathering up his notes for the debrief.

"Election law isn't my area of expertise, Mel, you know that."

"No, but you're a lawyer. I figured you could at least point me in the right direction."

"Have you tried the Secretary of State's office?"

"I'm not sure they'd be able to help."

"Why not?"

"It's a long story."

"Give me the short version. I've got a meeting to get to."

There was a pause on the line.

36

"I need to get Shep elected mayor."

"Shep your dog?"

"Yeah."

Bryce rubbed his eyes with a thumb and forefinger. This was exactly the kind of harebrained thing that went on in a small town. Proof, if any were needed, that his decision not to relocate to Fossett had been the right one.

"Why?"

"Things have been tough around here since the lumber mill closed. I was thinking that having a dog for a mayor might give the place a boost."

And now you want my help. How ironic.

Bryce heard a knock at the door; his team was waiting in the hallway.

"Make him an honorary mayor; that way you won't need an election." He snapped his briefcase shut. "Problem solved."

"I can't do that," Melanie said.

"Why not? As long as it's generally agreeable."

"Yeah, well . . . What if it isn't?"

"Ah. Then I guess you do have a problem."

"So, can you help me?"

Bryce took a deep breath. The truth was, he'd never gotten over his ex-wife and the temptation to say yes was powerful. The problem was that Melanie had a way of coming up with plans that sounded simple but invariably required more work than either she or anyone else had foreseen. It wasn't that her ideas were bad, necessarily — as dopey as this one sounded, it might even have some merit — but he knew that whatever she asked him for now would grow into a commitment of time and energy that he felt ill prepared to deal with. Maybe if things were different — if he were different — he'd be able to keep his distance, but Bryce was still too much in love with her to risk it. He glanced toward the door. Asa was giving him the signal to hurry up.

Oh, what the hell . . .

"Let me check it out and get back to you."

"Great! Can you do it by tomorrow? I'm sorta pressed for time."

"Tomorrow?"

"Pleeease. You know I wouldn't ask if it wasn't important."

Bryce shook his head, already kicking himself for not turning her down flat. He had clients to see and motions to file; he didn't have time to deal with some cocka-mamie scheme.

Then again, how long would it really take to find the information she needed? It wasn't even as if he'd have to do the work himself; this could easily be handed off to one of the paras. The important thing was to get Melanie off the phone so he could get to the debrief.

"Fine," he said. "I'll find out as much as I can, but no promises, understood?"

"No promises. Got it. You're an angel."

The four team members jostled one another like overgrown schoolboys as they headed for the conference room. Released from the grueling schedule that had ruled their waking hours for eight long months, they were flush with victory and impressed with their own success. Asa Conroy, whose encyclopedic knowledge of obscure legal precedents had won the day in court, punched Bryce in the arm.

"This your first debrief, Mac?"

Bryce elbowed him away, annoyed by the muscle cramp the guy's jab had provoked.

"I hear they used to hold these things at a strip club," Asa said. "The team members got free lap dances. Now all you get is an attaboy and one of the old man's cigars."

Bryce shook his head; Asa's tasteless comments would not be missed. He felt a shove from behind.

"Too bad he isn't giving out new cars, right, MacDonald?"

"Yeah," Asa said. "You're in the big leagues now; our clients want to know we're worth what they're paying us. Driving an old car like that makes you look like a loser."

"At least it's paid for," Bryce said, collecting high fives from the others.

Asa's face darkened.

"Why don't you go back to the DA's office where you belong?"

Bryce ignored the dig. Asa could talk all he wanted to about fitting in and looking the part of a high-priced attorney, but they both knew that the only things that counted around there were results. By that measure, Asa was on much shakier ground than he was.

The conference room was down the hall on the left. As their team turned the corner, the four men slowed to a crawl.

A woman was lounging in one of the visitors' chairs outside Fred Norcross's office. In a red silk suit, her long legs crossed under a too-short skirt and her dark hair spilling carelessly down her shoulders, Sofia Cardoza looked like a jungle cat on the prowl. She looked up and smiled.

"Well, hello, Bryce," she purred.

Bryce felt his face flush. In the months after his divorce, he'd stupidly allowed himself to tumble into Sofia's bed — a mistake he'd regretted ever since. Fortunately, it had happened just before she was chosen to serve out the remaining term of a state supreme court justice, giving him a convenient excuse to avoid any further entanglement. Since her term had expired, he'd been making a special effort to avoid her. The last thing he wanted was to start up where the two of them had left off.

"Hello, Judge. How are you?"

"Please," she said. "It's just 'Sofia' now."

She stood up, ignoring his outstretched hand, and gave him a more-than-friendly kiss.

"Congratulations on your win," she said, running a hand down his tie. "Very impressive."

As she drew back, Bryce caught the stunned expression on his team members' faces. The encounter might have been awkward, but Sofia's interest in him had apparently boosted his standing in their eyes.

Norcross's admin stepped into the hall.

"Judge Cardoza? Mr. Norcross will see you now."

"Thank you," Sofia said. "I'll be right there."

She lowered her voice.

"This shouldn't take long. Why don't you stick around? We could have a drink."

"I'd love to, but I've got this debrief," he

said, motioning toward the conference room. "Some other time, maybe?"

"Of course," she said. "Whenever you're ready."

Sofia turned and headed into Norcross's office, brushing past the others as she went. Bryce gave Asa a broad smile, relishing the look of naked envy on his face. No doubt, he thought, the guy would find some way to retaliate, but for the moment, it felt one hundred percent worth it.

The earthy aroma of Padróns still clung to his clothing as Bryce walked out of the office that afternoon. The debrief had gone well, he thought, the sting from any critical comments having vanished in a pleasant haze of blue smoke. On the whole, he felt his prospects at Norcross Daniels had never been better.

There was a Jaguar dealership around the corner; Bryce must have walked by it a hundred times without stopping. Living downtown, he seldom drove his car to work, and it was hard to justify paying that much for something he rarely used. Nevertheless, Asa's comment had started him thinking. Might some clients judge his worth as a counselor by the amount of money he spent? He already knew there were some at

Norcross Daniels who questioned his loyalties. What if Bryce's thrifty ways were really evidence of his inability to embrace the switch from prosecuting on the public's dime to defending on a blank check? As he approached the dealership, he decided to slow down and take a look.

A solitary salesman was pacing the showroom expectantly. Bryce groaned. He didn't want to be harangued by an eager beaver, especially when he wasn't even sure he was in the market. If only there'd been another customer inside, he thought, he could walk in without feeling exposed.

"Looking for some new wheels?"

Bryce turned and saw Glen Wheatley approaching. Glen was his ex-boss — the most senior assistant district attorney in the local office and one of the hardest-working prosecutors in the state. Having Glen for a mentor had been the best part of his tenure at the DA's office.

"Not sure," he said. "What do you think?"

Wheatley glanced at the shiny red F-TYPE in the window.

"It's a good-looking car," he said. "The dark side must be paying you well."

Bryce grinned.

"It does have its compensations. What are you doing out in the fresh air? Somebody open the cage door?"

"Actually, I was just heading over to your office. I'm glad I caught you."

"What's up?"

"Jesse Lee Colton escaped from prison last night."

Icy fingers clutched at Bryce's heart. Two years ago, he'd prosecuted Colton for the torture and murder of three people whose only crime had been crossing the man's path. The trial and conviction had been the high point of Bryce's career with the DA, but its aftermath was unnerving. At sentencing, an enraged Colton had charged the judge's bench, vowing to kill him and every member of the prosecution team once he regained his freedom. It wasn't the first time Bryce had received a death threat, but the nature of the man's crimes and the specificity with which he'd spelled out his intentions had been enough to give him nightmares. For almost a year, every creaking door, every unexpected footfall, every strange noise in the dark had sent his heart galloping. Only the assurance that Colton was in one of the most secure facilities in the nation had allowed Bryce to regain his equilibrium.

And now the man had escaped.

"Of course, he could be halfway to Mexico

by now," Wheatley said, "but Judge Trainor's been given a twenty-four-hour guard and I've advised the other members of the prosecution team to lay low until we find him. I suggest you do the same."

Bryce licked his lips. Joking about the dark side was one thing, but there really were attorneys in town — some of them members of his own firm — who thought the guys on the opposing team were in service to the devil. He had no wish to remind them where he'd come from. And what about their clients? When people stepped into the lobby at Norcross Daniels, they believed their troubles were over; they didn't want to hear about lowlifes like Jesse Lee Colton. If word got out that a convicted murderer was gunning for one of the firm's attorneys, business as usual would grind to a halt, Bryce's caseload would dry up, and any chance he might have had to move up the ranks would be gone.

He rubbed a hand across his mouth.

"I-I'm not sure I can."

"What?"

"It's hard to explain."

Wheatley gave him a hard look, then slowly shook his head.

"Well, it's up to you," he said. "But if it was me, I'd get the hell out of Dodge."

Bryce walked away in an altered state of consciousness, hypervigilant to any sight or sound that was out of the ordinary. Every person he passed looked like an assassin; every corner he turned held an ambush ready to spring. As he waited for the walk signal at Sixth and Yamhill, he stopped and took a deep breath, trying to get a grip. If he hadn't run into Glen Wheatley, he told himself, he'd never have known about Jesse Lee Colton. Chances were, the guy would be back behind bars within hours, if he wasn't there already. Acting like a scared rabbit wouldn't do anything but make him miserable.

By the time he reached his building, Bryce's panic had subsided. He checked his mailbox in the lobby and scooped up his newspaper, checking the front page as he waited for the elevator. Sure enough, Colton's escape had made the front page. The door opened and Bryce stepped inside, tucking the paper under his arm. Reading the article would only make things worse and there was probably nothing in it that he didn't already know. He heard footsteps coming closer and his next-door neighbor stepped inside.

Curtis Young was a jock — not terribly bright, but affable and easygoing. As far as

Bryce could tell, he spent most of his time at the gym. When the doors closed, the two of them traded sports news until they got to the fourth floor. Bryce stepped out first and started hunting for his key.

"Oh, hey," Curtis said as he passed him. "Did your brother ever get hold of you?"

Bryce had three sisters — two older, one younger — but no brother of any age. His throat felt suddenly dry.

"My brother?"

"Yeah. He was up here looking for you this morning — someone must have buzzed him in. I told him you usually got home around six or seven. Hope that's okay."

"Sure . . . fine," Bryce said, struggling to control the tremor in his voice. "Thanks for letting me know."

CHAPTER 4

Walt's delivery box held pumpkin muffins and cranberry scones that morning. As Melanie set them in her display case, she could hear Shep off in the corner munching his own treat.

"It's pumpkin today," Walt said, taking a seat. "Mae thought Shep would enjoy a taste of the season."

"Looks like it's a hit." She checked the smashed brownies sitting untouched in her display case. "Unlike the Beavertails."

"Yeah, it's hard to eat something that looks like it came off a rodent's heinie." Walt took a sip of his coffee. "Have you heard anything from that lawyer friend of yours?"

Melanie took out a towel and started wiping down the already clean counter.

"Not yet."

She hoped Walt wouldn't press her for details. The fact was, she'd only just called Bryce the day before. With time running out until Election Day, she knew it was important to get the information quickly, but she just hadn't been able to make the call. Now she was worried that the whole thing had been a mistake. What if Bryce never called her back? Promising help and then not delivering it would be the perfect form of retaliation. After all, why should he save the town that had taken her away from him?

She never should have made that offer. Why hadn't she thought her plan through before calling the meeting? Even now, she couldn't explain it. Melanie wasn't even sure the town needed legal advice in order to hold an election. Had she just been looking for an excuse to contact her ex-husband? She wished he'd just hurry and call her back so she could stop thinking about him.

Walt was studying her over his coffee.

"So, how is Bryce?"

She kept her head down, feeling her face color. Melanie hadn't told anyone the name of their legal benefactor, and having Walt guess his identity was embarrassing.

"I'm not sure," she said, scrubbing the counter more vigorously. "We only talked for a minute."

"Long enough to get you riled up, though."

She shoved the towel back under the counter.

"I'm not riled up."

"Oh." He nodded. "Thanks for telling me."

Melanie sighed. Snapping at Walt wasn't going to help anything; contacting Bryce had been her idea, not his. She just wished the call hadn't unnerved her so much. When their divorce was final and everything had been settled, she'd told herself to put any lingering doubts aside; whether or not her choice to stay in Fossett had been the right one was irrelevant. The important thing was to move on, and the only way to do that was to sever any ties she had with her ex-husband. Better to have nothing more to do with him than to waste time second-guessing herself. And then, in one desperate moment, she'd undone all her good intentions.

"Maybe I am upset," she said. "I mean, I know he's busy, but it can't be that difficult to get the information I asked him for. He probably just passed it off to one of the paralegals and forgot about it."

"Well, I'm glad to hear you're not getting your hopes up. I like Bryce well enough, but I wouldn't want to see you get hurt."

She shook her head.

"Believe me, I'm not interested in getting back together with Bryce, and I'm sure he isn't, either."

When Walt had gone, Melanie put his cup in the sink and went out to wipe down the table. In spite of what she'd said, she found the thought of Bryce fobbing her problem off on an assistant vaguely offensive. Surely, taking a few minutes to research a simple question wasn't too much to ask from someone who'd once vowed to love and cherish her for a lifetime. But then, she thought, it wouldn't be the first time he'd lied to her, would it?

The morning crowd began to filter in, distracting her from her tetchy mood. As Melanie took orders and made drinks, she reminded herself that the important thing now was to get the answer she needed, not whether Bryce had actually done the work himself. In some ways, it might even be better if he'd had someone else do it for him. That way, she wouldn't feel any extra obligation toward him. Walt wasn't the only one who didn't want to see her get hurt again.

The last of the coffee drinkers had just taken a seat when the bell on Melanie's front door jangled and Selma bustled in, bright-eyed and beaming.

"It's working!"

Selma looked like she'd sprinted the four blocks from the Fossett House to get there. Her hair was a mass of frazzled curls, and the cold weather had left her cheeks an impressive shade of pink.

Melanie frowned. "What's working?"

"Shep," Selma said breathlessly. "The election. It's working."

"Is this about the thing in the paper?"

There'd been an article in Wednesday's edition of *The Fossett Informer* about their meeting last Sunday. Perhaps another paper had picked it up.

"Must have been," Selma said, nodding eagerly. "When the man showed up last night, he said he'd heard about Shep and wanted to check things out for himself."

Melanie felt a flutter of excitement. Until that moment, her plan hadn't seemed quite real even to her. Now the thought of her hometown filling with people anxious to meet its canine mayor made her pulse quicken.

"But if you've got a guest, what are you doing here?"

"Oh. Our brochure says we serve complimentary coffee with breakfast."

"You do?"

"No. That's why I had to come over here.

I told him to take a seat in the common room and I snuck out the back door."

Melanie sighed and looked heavenward. This right here was the problem with Fossett. No matter how many improvements the town made, somebody always had to make sure they were put to good use, and a remodeled bed-and-breakfast that didn't serve breakfast was nothing but an old house with strangers living in it.

"Okay. No problem. I'll get you some to take back."

She grabbed a carafe from under the counter and took it over to the coffee urns.

"Does he want regular or decaf?"

"I forgot to ask. Sorry."

"Why don't we make it regular? If he asks for decaf, give me a call and I'll bring it over while you serve breakfast."

Selma's gaze slipped away.

"Yeah, breakfast . . ."

"You *do* have something to feed him for breakfast, don't you?"

"I *did,* but there's been nobody there but me, and you know how I get when I'm bored. I guess I must have eaten it." Her face brightened. "I've still got some Beavertails."

Melanie tried not to be upset. It wasn't really Selma's fault; the people who'd given her the job didn't know any more about running a B and B than she did. She couldn't help thinking of Walt's comment, though. Maybe he was right. Maybe there weren't enough "normal" people left in Fossett to turn the place around.

"Tell you what," she said, closing the top on the carafe. "I'll give you some of Walt's baked goods for now. Just make sure you go by the grocery store before tomorrow."

They stepped behind the counter and Melanie gave Selma a box to carry the pastries in. This was just a hiccup, she told herself as she reached for a muffin. A tiny bump on the road to a better future. If Shep's story could bring one person into town before the election, imagine how many would show up once he was the mayor. This was definitely going to work.

The bell on the front door rang.

"I'll be right with you!" she said. "Ow!"

Selma had taken her arm in a death grip.

"Atsthay imhay."

"What?" she hissed, trying to pry the woman's fingers loose.

"Him. The guy who checked in."

"Oh."

Melanie smoothed the wrinkles from her apron, anxious to make a good impression on their new customer. As she stepped out from behind the pastry display, however, the smile froze on her face.

Bryce had changed since she'd seen him last. The bland attire of a newly minted lawyer had been replaced by a fashionable grey suit, Italian loafers, and a knee-length camel hair coat; his hair was skinned back in a style that banished the waves that once fell across his forehead. Her first impression was that he looked good — very good — but on second inspection, she realized that something was off.

The expensive suit looked slept in and the handmade shoes were lacking a shine. There were dark circles under his eyes, too, and a tightness around his mouth that told her he was under stress. And there was something else, something that all the expensive clothes and designer haircuts in the world couldn't disguise, something that maybe only she would notice: Bryce MacDonald was scared.

"Hey, Mel."

"Hey, Bryce."

Selma was watching their exchange, open-mouthed.

"You two know each other?"

Melanie nodded.

"Bryce is the lawyer I told you about. He's agreed to help us find a way to make Shep the mayor."

"I'm also her ex-husband," he said. "But I guess we don't need to talk about that."

"No," Melanie said. "We don't."

Bryce looked at Selma.

"I hope you don't mind. I saw you leave and figured I'd just save you the trouble of bringing the coffee back."

"No, not at all." She looked at the carafe in her hands. "You want me to pour you some?"

He glanced at Melanie.

"Any chance I could get an espresso instead? I've been running on empty for a couple of days."

"Sure," she said. "Have a seat and I'll bring it out."

While Bryce found a table, Melanie grabbed a cup and started grinding the beans.

How dare he just show up, uninvited? All it would have taken was a phone call.

Selma put the carafe on the counter and sidled up beside her.

"I can't believe you let him get away," she whispered. "I would not have given that man up without a fight. Unless he was gay, of course."

She turned and watched Bryce settle into his seat.

"Nope," she said. "Not even then."

Melanie was waiting for the water to heat.

"Let's just say it was complicated and leave it at that."

"Oh. Well, okay." Selma picked up the carafe. "I, uh, guess I'll just take this back with me then."

She gave Bryce a last lingering look and headed out the door.

Melanie pulled the espresso and walked it over to Bryce. It hit the table with a thud.

"What are you doing here?"

He took a sip.

"Ahh, that's good. Thanks." He set the cup back down. "I got the information you asked for."

"You could have called, you know. Saved yourself a trip."

"I could have, but I needed some fresh air."

He glanced at the dog in the corner.

"Is that Shep? He's really filled out since you got him."

Bryce held out his hand.

"Hey, buddy. Remember me?"

Shep raised his head and gave him the once-over. As a rule, Melanie's border collie was quick to greet all comers, but there were times when he hung back, waiting for a sign that the interloper was harmless. For whatever reason, he'd decided that this new arrival didn't meet with his approval.

"Hmm," Bryce said. "Not very friendly for a politician. You'll have to work on that."

"Funny," she said. "He gets along just fine with most people."

Bryce shrugged and took another sip of coffee.

"I like what you've done with this place."

Melanie was finding it hard to maintain her sense of outrage. Bryce was only there because she'd asked him for a favor, after all. She sighed and took a seat.

"Thanks."

"Wasn't there a café across the street?"

"It's gone," she said. "Along with half the other businesses in town. We need to get more people to move here."

"Hence the whole 'Shep for mayor' thing."

"Right."

He took another sip.

"Think it'll work?"

"Honestly? I have no idea. At this point, I'm willing to try anything."

"Well, I hate to tell you this, but if you're determined to do something by Election Day, you're running out of options."

"Yeah, I was afraid of that."

"However," he said. "I think I have an idea that'll work and I should have a preliminary campaign schedule hammered out by to-night."

"Campaign schedule?" Melanie stared. "What for?"

Bryce's look was incredulous.

"How do you expect to get Shep elected if you don't have a campaign?"

"I don't know," she said, feeling flustered. "I hadn't really thought about it. Does it matter?"

"Of course it matters. The more professional Shep's campaign is, the more the people around here will get behind him."

Melanie sat back. It felt as if things were moving too fast. It had been less than a week since she'd even gotten the idea.

"But I don't know anything about running a political campaign."

"I do," Bryce said.

"*You* want to run Shep's campaign? What about your job?"

"I've got some vacation time accrued, *and* I've got political experience."

She smirked.

"Being the class president at Mountain Ridge High School doesn't count."

"The same principles apply." He grinned. "Come on. It'll be fun."

Melanie paused. The truth was, she'd been a little worried about the election. Ever since the town meeting, people had been telling her that Rod Blakely was going around trying to sell himself as the next mayor. Nevertheless, she wasn't convinced that working with her ex-husband was a good idea.

"I don't know . . ."

"Look," he said. "Election Day is just over a week away. We can keep from killing each other for that long, can't we?"

She looked away. It wasn't killing each other that she was worried about.

"Maybe," she said. "But only if Shep agrees."

"Of course!" He turned and smiled at the dog in the corner. "The two of us are gonna make a great team. Right, Shep?"

The collie, who'd been checking his dog bed for any overlooked crumbs, did not respond.

"Hey," Bryce said. "What's with the cold shoulder?"

Melanie shrugged.

"He gets like this sometimes — it took him a while to trust anyone after his first owners got rid of him. Don't worry about it."

"Okay," he said, setting his cup aside. "Tell you what then. I'll go back to my room and put together a plan for the campaign.

When do you get off?"

"We close at six."

"Perfect. We can discuss it over dinner. I'll stop by the store and meet you at your place at seven. How does stir-fry sound?"

The offer was tempting. Bryce had always been a good cook, and fixing dinner at the end of the workday was one of Melanie's least favorite chores. Nevertheless, she'd worked too hard to close that chapter of her life to reopen it for the sake of convenience.

"Seven is fine," she said, "but I'll make dinner."

"But —"

Melanie shut down his protest with a look.

"Please, Bryce, for both our sakes. Let's not go down that road again."

He threw his hands up in surrender.

"Got it. No problem. I'll see you at seven."

CHAPTER 5

Bryce walked into his hotel room and closed
the door. Seeing Melanie had left him
stunned, rattled, and emotionally drained.
He'd thought he was over her, that time and
distance had made it possible to be in the
same room with her without it tearing him
up inside. Now he realized how wrong he'd
been. He sat down and put his head in his
hands. How on earth was he going to get
through dinner?

I shouldn't have come.

The worst part was seeing how little their
meeting had affected her. Even when she
was caught off guard, the only thing she
seemed upset about was that he'd come in
person to give her the information rather
than making a call. This was exactly what
he'd feared: that it had been easier for Melanie to get over him than the other way
around.

Bryce shook his head, trying to summon

the anger that would stop him from brooding. What difference did it make which one of them had been hurt more? Just look at where she was: living in some backwater, working herself to death in a pointless job while the town crumbled around her. Meanwhile, he was living in a vibrant city and making a ton of money doing a job that most guys would kill for. Even a fool could see which one of them had made the right decision. He wasn't the one who should be upset — she was.

When his phone rang, Bryce's first thought was that it was Melanie calling to cancel, and his pang of disappointment put the lie to any outrage he'd been able to summon. He took the iPhone out of his coat pocket, relieved to see Glen Wheatley's number.

"I got your message," Glen said. "What's up?"

Bryce had left him a voice mail the night before about the man at the condo.

"My neighbor saw a guy in our building yesterday who said he was looking for me. Told him he was my brother. Problem is, I don't have a brother."

"You get a description of the guy?"

"Sorry. I was so spooked I didn't think to ask."

"Crap."

"It may be nothing, but I thought I'd take your advice and get out of town for a while. I'm staying at a B and B down in Fossett."

"Good. That's one less headache I have to deal with."

"Any word on Colton?"

"Nope. The hotline's been busy, but nothing's panned out yet. Right now, we're just waiting for Vance to come out of surgery."

"What?"

Vance Rowland had been Bryce's co-counsel on Colton.

"You didn't know?"

"No. What happened?"

"He was shot — sitting at the dinner table with Bev and the kids. Whoever did it must have been hiding in the bushes outside his house."

"Is he okay?"

"He's alive. Doc said if the bullet had gone in half a centimeter higher, the guy'd be on a slab."

"Witnesses?"

"Nobody saw nothin'."

Bryce ran a hand over his mouth and tugged at his lower lip. He'd almost convinced himself the decision to leave town had been too hasty, that the man Curtis talked to had simply wandered into the wrong building by mistake. Now that explanation seemed a whole lot less likely.

"I can increase the patrols around your building in case he comes back," Glen said. "In the meantime, stay where you are. I'll call you if anything changes."

"Yeah, okay. Thanks."

As Bryce hung up, he felt his whole body start to shake. A minute ago, he'd been thinking he should just go home, but the attack on Vance changed everything. It could have been a random act — the method didn't really sound like Colton — but the timing was suspicious. Wheatley was right. It was smarter just to stay where he was for the time being.

He took a deep breath and slowly let it out, trying to calm his mind and body. At least he had something to do while he waited. Putting together Shep's campaign schedule would keep him busy for now, and if Colton was still at large tomorrow he and Melanie could start putting it into action. Being with her might not be easy, but it was safer than going home. As he took out his computer and got to work, it occurred to him that leaving for Fossett might literally have saved his life.

■ ■ ■ ■

Melanie's bungalow was one among dozens of nearly identical houses that lined the serpentine streets of Fossett's residential area. Built for timber company employees around the turn of the last century, the homes had been erected as the need arose, with none of the planning and forethought that made getting into and out of a modern subdivision quick and easy; the distance from Fossett House — about a mile as the crow flies — had taken him almost seven minutes to drive. If there was ever a need to evacuate the town in an emergency, he thought, some folks might not make it out in time.

Bryce parked at the curb, grabbed the bottle of wine he'd bought on the way there, and hurried through a cold drizzle to the front door. The sound of the doorbell prompted a canine uproar inside and he could hear Melanie trying to shush the dog, to little effect. As the door opened, she was bent over, holding Shep by the collar.

"I've got him," she said. "Come on in."

Bryce stepped across the threshold and Melanie took the dog's head in her hands.

"Don't be rude, Shep. Bryce is here to

help us."

The collie delivered a final *woof* and slunk off to his dog bed in the corner.

"Sorry about that," she said. "We don't get a lot of company."

"At least he's a good watchdog."

Bryce held out the bottle.

"I took a chance and brought red. It was Gunderson's finest, so don't get your hopes up."

Melanie looked at the wine bottle like it was a dangerous animal.

"It doesn't mean anything," he said. "Just a thank-you for having me over."

She reached out and accepted it gingerly.

"I'll set it out to breathe. There's a hook by the door for your coat."

Bryce hung his coat up and swatted away a few drops of rain while Shep eyed him from across the room. He knew it had been a long time since they'd seen each other, but he hadn't expected Melanie's dog to be so wary of him. He wondered what the problem was.

"How ya doing, boy?"

The collie lowered his ears and growled softly.

Melanie bustled back into the room.

"Okay," she said. "Wine's aerating and dinner will be ready in ten."

Bryce nodded toward the dog bed.

"I don't think Shep likes me."

"Of course he likes you," she said. "He's just tired. The Stubbses' goats got out this afternoon and he had to get them back into their pens."

Bryce glanced at the dog glowering at him from the corner. Shep didn't look tired to him.

"So," she said. "Have you figured out how to hold an election?"

"Yes and no. There isn't really enough time between now and Election Day to hold an official election. Oregon law requires it to be vote by mail, and we can't even get a list of registered voters by then."

Melanie's face fell.

"I thought you said —"

"Hold on. What you *can* do is hold a referendum."

She made a face.

"What's the difference?"

"A referendum is just a single-vote issue *and* it doesn't have to meet the same requirements as a regular election does. Plus, if it doesn't pass, you're not stuck with an open seat to fill. You just have to make sure that at least two-thirds of the electorate vote," he said. "We get ballots printed, set up voting booths in a central location, and when everything is counted, we're done."

Melanie thought it over.

"But what if there's more than one candidate?"

Bryce shook his head.

"Can't do that."

"I don't know," she said. "Let me think about it."

"Fine," he said. "But at this point, it's that or nothing."

She checked her watch.

"Listen, we've still got a few minutes until dinner's ready. Would you mind if I show you a few tricks that Shep can do? I thought it might give you some ideas for how to use him in the campaign."

"You mean like rolling over, shaking hands?"

Melanie laughed. "Way better than that. This boy is super smart."

She glanced at the dog lying on his bed.

"Shep," she said. "Want to play fetch?"

The collie jumped to attention.

"Border collies get bored easily, so I give him challenges to try and keep him from developing bad habits." She waved a hand, indicating the tooth-marked furniture. "One of the things I've done is teach him the names of his toys. At this point, he's got a vocabulary of about two hundred and fifty words."

"You're kidding!"

"Nope. Watch this." She turned. "Shep, fetch the blue ball."

The collie trotted across the room to a pile of toys in the opposite corner, carefully picked out a small blue ball, and dropped it at Melanie's feet.

"Wow," Bryce said.

"Hold on," she said. "Shep, fetch the yellow rabbit."

Once again, the dog went to the pile of toys. This time, Bryce noticed how Shep carefully avoided a blue rabbit before returning with the requested item.

"Impressive."

"Dogs don't see colors quite as well as we do — especially reds and greens — but what he can't find by color he generally knows by shape. And of course, everything has a name. Shep," she said, "fetch Mickey Mouse."

Seconds later, a plush Mickey was deposited at her feet. Bryce laughed out loud.

"That's amazing."

She grinned. "I know, right? I thought if we could find a way to work some of this stuff into the campaign, it would really get people excited."

A buzzer went off in the kitchen.

"I have to go take up dinner. Why don't you play with him till I get back?"

As Melanie disappeared into the kitchen, Bryce turned and smiled at Shep.

"All right," he said. "Let's try this together, shall we?"

He surveyed the mountain of toys that had colonized the other half of the living room.

"Shep, fetch the Pink Panther."

The dog cocked his head but stayed where he was.

"The Pink Panther," Bryce said, making sure to enunciate clearly.

Shep sat down and scratched behind an ear.

"Over there." He pointed. "Fetch. The. Pink. Panther."

Shep yawned and stretched out on the floor.

"Okaaaay," Bryce said, glancing back at the pile. "How about the carrot? Do you know what a carrot is? No? What about the fire truck? Is that too hard for you?"

The collie rolled onto his side.

Bryce pursed his lips. First the growl and now this. What was going on? Shep had been standoffish at the coffee shop, too. Was he just shy around men, or was there something more going on?

Bryce took a moment to examine his surroundings, hoping to find a clue to the dog's behavior. In addition to the large, fur-covered dog bed and the enormous pile of toys, there was a photo of Shep and Melanie at a Halloween party dressed as Romeo and Juliet, an "I love my border collie" pillow on an easy chair, a plaster cast of Shep's front paws on the coffee table, and an oil painting over the sofa that looked like Shep's head on the body of a man wearing a tuxedo. No wonder the dog didn't like him, Bryce thought. Shep wasn't just a dog; he was a baby, best pal, and boyfriend all wrapped up in one big, fluffy package.

He looked at the dog, still stretched out on the floor.

"Hey, pal," he said quietly. "I can see you've got a pretty sweet deal going on, but I didn't ask to come here. So, why don't you do yourself a favor and get that chip off your furry little shoulder?"

Shep looked away for a moment, then slowly rolled back over and got up. He turned toward the pile, lowered his head, and trotted across the room, his gaze riveted on the toys.

"Good dog," Bryce said. "I knew you'd see it my way."

The Pink Panther, however, remained

untouched, as did the carrot and the fire truck. Instead, Shep began to dig through the pile, throwing toys in his wake like a terrier pursuing a rat. When he found what he was after, he lifted it carefully, then trotted back and dropped it just out of reach.

Bryce looked at the toy on the floor.

"Nice try, Einstein, but that's not what I asked for."

It was a little man, dressed in a blue suit and a tiny red tie. Its face and hands were made of pink felt, its hair a dozen loops of brown yarn. As Bryce watched, Shep put a forepaw on the little man's chest, took its head carefully between his teeth, and yanked. Stitches popped and felt tore as the doll's head came off. Shep dropped it next to the decapitated body and stared at him.

"So," Bryce said. "That's the way it's going to be, huh?"

"That's the way what's going to be?"

Man and dog looked up as Melanie came back into the room.

"Oh no!" she said. "What happened to Mr. Stuffy?"

At once, Shep threw himself on the ground, whining pitifully as he tried to nose the pieces back together.

"My poor baby." She scooped up the mangled doll and gave the collie a hug.

"Don't worry. Mommy will fix it."

She turned to Bryce. "What happened?"

"Beats me. One minute we were playing, and the next minute Mr. Stuffy's head just . . . came off."

"Well, I guess it doesn't matter," she said doubtfully, examining the pieces in her hand. "And at least you got a chance to see what he can do."

"Absolutely," Bryce said as he and the collie locked eyes. "I think I understand Shep perfectly."

CHAPTER 6

Dinner was over and the dishes had been put away before they got back to the subject of the campaign. So far, Melanie thought, things had gone better than expected. There'd been no awkward silences, no mention of past grievances, not even any hints about trying again. In fact, the entire evening had felt more like getting together with an old school chum than an ex-husband. She should be happy, she told herself. So, why was she upset?

Maybe it was the shock of seeing how much he'd changed. It wasn't just the clothes and the hair; Bryce seemed a lot less . . . dejected than he'd been the last time she saw him. Not that she'd expected him to pine away forever, but no woman wanted to think that a man she'd once loved had gotten over her. It made her feel prickly and resentful.

As Bryce set his plans for the campaign

out on her dining room table, Melanie felt her lips tighten. He'd done all that work without even asking her, and now he was expecting her to just step aside. Did he think that because he was a big-time lawyer now he could just show up and take charge? As he closed his briefcase, her stomach began to churn.

Time to nip this in the bud.

"I don't think having you as Shep's campaign manager is going to work."

He looked up.

"Oh?"

She shook her head.

"You don't really know the people around here and I'm not sure how they'll feel about a stranger coming in and trying to run things."

Bryce bit his upper lip, something Melanie remembered that he did when he was feeling conflicted.

Okay, here comes the "I know what's best for you" speech.

"Yeah, I can see that."

He patted the folder in front of him.

"So, do you want any of this? I could just leave it here."

"Um, sure," she said, feeling wrongfooted. "I guess it wouldn't hurt to take a look."

Why was he being so agreeable all of a sudden? He'd seemed so eager this afternoon. Without someone to push back against, Melanie felt herself losing momentum.

"I'm not sure about making it a referendum, either," she said. "I mean, the whole reason we decided to have an election was because Rod Blakely said it wouldn't be fair if Shep was the only candidate. A one-question referendum seems pretty much like the same thing to me."

"Is Blakely the guy who wants to run against Shep?"

"Yeah."

"But I thought the whole point was to have a *dog* as the mayor."

"It is, but fairness matters to people around here. They feel as if their way of life has been destroyed by rules they had no say in."

"Of course, I get that. So, what do you want to do?"

Melanie paused. What *did* she want to do? The whole point of calling Bryce in the first place had been to ask his advice. Why was she so reluctant now to take it? Still, the thought of simply turning everything over to him rankled.

"Could we have two referendums on the

same ballot?"

"You mean like two separate questions: 'Make Shep the mayor?' or 'Make Rod the mayor?' "

"Right."

He frowned thoughtfully.

"I should think so."

"If we did that, then the rest would be like you said before: get ballots printed, set up voting booths, let everyone vote. We'd just have two questions for people to decide on instead of one."

"What if Rod Blakely wins? Are you sure you want to take that chance?"

Melanie laughed.

"Don't worry, he won't."

"But if he does?"

"Well, if he does, he does. But believe me, he's not going to."

"All right. Sounds like a plan."

She smiled. Getting everything out in the open and settled had put her in a better frame of mind.

"Thanks for the help," she said. "I really appreciate it."

Without thinking, Melanie laid her hand on his arm. She'd only meant it as a friendly gesture, but the sensation was electric. Feeling his body heat, the way the hair on his forearm contrasted with the smoothness of his skin, the power of the underlying muscle, made her heart race. She realized suddenly just how long it had been since she'd touched a man — any man — and snatched her hand away.

If Bryce had noticed her discomfort, however, it didn't show.

"No problem," he said. "I came here to help, not tell you what to do."

"Great. Wonderful," she said, feeling annoyed again.

Since when is he such a cool customer?

"Can I make a suggestion, though?" he said. "Since it's not a statewide election, why don't you hold it on Saturday instead of Election Day? You'll get a bigger turnout that way."

"But that'd give us three fewer days and we don't have much time as it is."

"How many people live in Fossett, a thousand?"

She shrugged.

"About that."

"Then the campaign shouldn't take that long. You could hold the vote a week from today and have the ballots counted and certified that night. If Fossett's in as bad shape as you say it is, then the sooner Shep gets into office the quicker your plan can do its work."

"I hadn't thought about that," she said. "Let me talk to Walt and see what he says."

"Okay. In the meantime, Ms. Campaign Manager, here's your playbook."

He handed her the folder containing the action plan for Shep's campaign.

"It's probably more than you need, under the circumstances, but it's always good to have a blueprint before you start."

Melanie raised a skeptical eyebrow as she lifted the cover. Was this really necessary? On the one hand, there was no way she was going to need all of this stuff. On the other hand, Bryce had gone to a lot of trouble to put the thing together. It would be rude not to at least take a look at it before he left.

As she began flipping through the pages and reading his action items, though, Melanie started to realize just how little she knew about actually running a campaign. There were sections on energizing voters, ensuring a good turnout, raising seed money, and attracting volunteers. By the time she'd reached the last page, she felt overwhelmed.

"Wow. This is impressive."

Maybe it wouldn't hurt to have Bryce stay and explain some of it to her, she thought. She only had a few days until the election, after all, and there were several action items in there that she hadn't even considered.

"Would you mind if we went over some of this stuff before you go? This is a lot to take in."

"Sure. We can do that."

She handed the folder back and Bryce laid it open on the table. Melanie took a seat on the other side, relieved to be putting some distance between them.

"Okay," he said. "The first thing you'll need to do is make up a list of likely voters."

"Easy," she said. "That'd be everyone."

"Are you sure? Remember, the referendum won't be valid without two-thirds of the people casting a ballot. Just because someone *can* vote in an election, that doesn't mean they *will.*"

She thought about that for a second. The fact was, Melanie had no idea what Fossett's voter turnout had been like in the past. She'd just assumed that everyone in town would show up to support Shep.

"Yeah, I guess you're right. But short of dragging everyone to the polls, how do we make sure they do?"

"Two ways," he said. "First, you find volunteers: people who will help get the word out about Shep's candidacy."

"No problem. I've had lots of people tell me they want to help."

"Good, you'll want to contact them as soon as possible. The second thing is, you have to ask for donations."

She shook her head.

"I can't do that. People in this town are already hurting."

"It doesn't have to be a lot," he said. "Even a dollar will do. The point is, once someone donates to a candidate, they're more likely to show up and vote for them."

"Huh. I didn't know that."

"Believe me," he said, "it works. If I were you, I'd put a star next to the names of likely voters who might contribute to Shep's campaign. The more people you can get money from, the better his chances will be."

"Shep's at the coffee shop every day greeting customers. I'm sure most of them will chip in."

Bryce grimaced and shook his head.

"I wouldn't recommend it," he said. "You don't want people to start wondering if you're trading political favors for good service."

"Oh, please," she scoffed. "What kind of political favors is a dog going to hand out? Besides, folks around here know me better than that."

"Are you sure? People can get funny about politics."

"But this isn't *politics* politics; it's just for fun."

"Don't fool yourself, Mel. It stopped being 'fun' the second you held that town meeting. I'll bet Rod Blakely is treating this election very seriously."

Melanie paused. Rod *had* been pretty agitated at the meeting. Plus, he was the one who'd brought up the whole fairness issue, and there were all those stories about his disparaging Shep's candidacy, too.

"So, what do I do?"

"Don't talk about politics at work," Bryce said. "If your customers ask about Shep's candidacy or how they can help, have them talk to one of your volunteers — or to me, if I'm still in town."

She licked her lips, reviewing the bullet points on the paper in front of her. The thought of having to do all that stuff by herself was daunting.

"Is that all?"

"Nope, there's one more thing. Shep needs to get out and ask for people's votes. It's called canvassing, and it's really important."

"How's he going to do that? I mean, he is smart, but he doesn't talk."

"Talking isn't mandatory, but walking through neighborhoods, calling on voters —

even shaking hands, if he'll do that — will help people form a positive opinion of him. At the same time, you — or whoever he's with — need to be asking for their support."

She sighed, realizing for the first time how much work the election would involve. How was she going to do all that and still keep the coffee shop running?

"Can we just skip the door-to-door stuff? I mean, it's getting pretty cold outside. Couldn't I just put an ad in the paper?"

"You could," Bryce said. "But it won't have the same impact. People want to feel that you're willing to work for their vote. If they think you're just phoning it in, they'll be put off."

Melanie slumped onto the table.

"This is hard."

"It's supposed to be. You don't win people over by doing what's easy. You have to be willing to do what's hard."

He closed the folder and pushed it across the table.

"Remember, the key to winning an election is showing voters that you don't take them for granted. Don't just buy ads, show up in person; don't just talk, listen; don't just assume they'll come out and vote, give them a reason to. If you and Shep do that, he really will be a shoo-in."

Bryce grinned.

"Look on the bright side: At least he's not running for a *real* political office."

Melanie looked across the room. Shep had dozed off and his legs were beginning to jerk fitfully. She wondered if he was dreaming of herding sheep.

"Why do you think Shep tore Mr. Stuffy's head off? I mean, it's obvious he did it on purpose. You don't think it has anything to do with the election, do you?"

"I don't see how it could. The campaign hasn't even started."

"Yeah, you're right. I just wish I knew why."

Melanie grabbed the folder and flipped it back open. Where was she going to find the time to do all this stuff? Kayla only worked part-time, and that was during the busiest part of the day when the shop really needed two people at the counter. Melanie might be able to get someone in temporarily, but that would take money she didn't have and she was already teetering on a thin financial edge. The plan she'd been expecting to save her town might just ruin her.

"What if I do all this and it still doesn't work?"

"You mean, what if Fossett goes down the

drain? Sorry," he said. "That was in poor taste."

"No, it's okay." She took a deep breath. "Better to laugh than cry, right?"

Melanie closed her eyes feeling weary to her bones. She'd been fighting to save her town for almost four years and things never seemed to get any better. At what point would it be enough?

"You look tired," he said.

"I *am* tired." She lifted her hand to cover a yawn. "It's been a long day."

"I'd better go, then." Bryce stood up. "There's a lot of work to do in a very short time. You won't be able to do it if you're exhausted."

Suddenly, the thought of being alone unnerved her and Melanie found herself close to tears. Even if she could get volunteers to help, even if Kayla agreed to work extra hours, she'd still have to make all the decisions herself. What if she made a mistake? What if she blew it and Rod Blakely *did* become the mayor? Fossett would be worse off than if she'd never done anything.

"Bryce, could you still be Shep's campaign manager, at least for a couple of days? You know, till I get the hang of it. I just don't think I can do all of this stuff alone."

"Sure, if you want me to."

Melanie almost sobbed in relief.

"Thank you." She leaned over and gave him a kiss. "You're an angel of mercy."

"Yep, that's me," he said, snapping his briefcase shut. "I'll order the ballots and file whatever paperwork is needed online. Do you think you can get someone to cover for you at work tomorrow?"

"Probably. Why?"

"We'll need to start canvassing as soon as possible."

She thought about that.

"Kayla will be there in the morning. I should be able to get someone to cover for me in the afternoon."

"Good," he said. "Now go to bed before you fall asleep on the couch."

Melanie giggled.

"You always hated when I did that."

"Yes, and I still would."

She walked him to the door.

"Thanks for coming."

"No problem." Bryce put on his coat. "I'll come by the shop in the morning and we'll start making the rounds. Once you see how canvassing is done, I think you'll feel more confident about the rest."

"Okay."

"And Mel?" He turned to face her. "I'm proud of you for trying to pull this off. I hope it works."

Melanie felt her chin dimple.

"Really?"

"Yes, really. Now get some rest."

CHAPTER 7

Bryce lay in bed the next morning, watching the shadows move slowly across his hotel room. The alarm had gone off half an hour ago, but he couldn't quite make himself get up. The time he'd spent at Melanie's the night before had both pleased and puzzled him. There'd been a few false starts, of course, and the Mr. Stuffy episode was awkward, but after that it was just like old times, the two of them teasing and flirting — she'd even kissed him. The more he thought about it, the more convinced he was that Melanie had changed her mind about getting back together. Now the question was, after everything that had happened, could they still make it work?

For the first few weeks after their divorce, Bryce had been stunned, unable to reconcile his new life with the one he'd been living only a few months before. Even now, he couldn't pinpoint the exact moment when things between them had gone off the rails. Their courtship was no more fraught than their friends', their arguments no more heated or destructive. Melanie talked about moving back to Fossett "someday," but there was never any time frame mentioned, and with law school to finish and bar exams looming, Bryce couldn't afford to worry about something that might never happen. Any inkling he might have had that a crisis was looming was put aside for the sake of expediency.

Then Melanie finished school and got a job she said she loved. The fact that it wasn't in her hometown seemed to be irrelevant, and Bryce thought the matter was settled. So it was a shock when he passed the bar and Melanie refused to stay in Portland. In spite of the lack of opportunities for him in Fossett, she dug in her heels, accusing him of lying to her about his willingness to relocate. After that, things unraveled quickly. When Bryce told her he'd accepted a job in the DA's office, it was the last straw.

That was one thing about Melanie that hadn't changed. Once she'd made up her mind about something, she refused to budge. It wasn't necessarily a bad thing, and her persistence in the face of misfortune was one of the things he admired about her, but trying to make her dog the mayor was pretty clearly a last-ditch effort. Even if Shep did become the mayor, there was no way that tourism alone was going to pull the town out of its tailspin. It did, however, leave the door open for him to try to persuade her to do the right thing. Once she saw how much work a campaign involved, Bryce was sure she'd shelve the whole "mayor Shep" thing and see that the best thing for her to do was to come back to Portland. There, she could find a better job, move into his condo, and the two of them could start over.

Bryce rolled out of bed and got dressed. No doubt, there'd be adjustments to make. They'd both been on their own for a few years and it would take a while to learn to live together again. The only real problem he could foresee was Shep. Melanie had spoiled the dog rotten, and if he was going to live in the condo they'd have to get him under control. Fortunately, Bryce had experience raising dogs. They were pack animals, quick to fall in line behind the alpha. Once Bryce showed him who was boss, the rest would be smooth sailing.

The line was nearly out the door by the time

he arrived at Ground Central. When Bryce walked in, Melanie was behind the counter pulling an espresso and Kayla was fetching pastries out of the display case. Shep, who'd been greeting customers, took one look at him and went back to his dog bed.

"Shep! Come back and say hello to Bryce."

"No, it's okay," he said. "Don't worry about it."

He stepped aside as another person got in line.

"Doesn't look like you'll be free to go canvassing anytime soon."

She shook her head.

"Not until this surge dies down, anyway."

"Anything I can do to help?"

Melanie wiped her hands on her apron and tested the steamer.

"Actually, if you could take Shep out for some exercise, that'd be great. He didn't get a chance to run his obstacle course this morning and I don't want him getting antsy while we're trying to talk to people."

Bryce smiled. Working with Shep one-on-one would be the perfect way to get their relationship sorted out.

"Great idea," he said. "Any place in particular I should take him?"

"There's a trail about five miles east of

here that Shep loves. It goes through a meadow and then down along the river. That should wear him out."

"Sounds good. Just tell me where his lead is and we'll leave you to it."

"Oh, you won't need one; Shep's a good heeler." She finished the latte and set it on the counter. "With any luck, I'll be ready to go by the time you two get back."

Taking the collie out without a lead didn't sound like a good idea to Bryce, but he'd already agreed and standing there arguing with her would pretty much negate his offer of help.

"Okay," he said. "We'll see you later."

Shep sat quietly in the back seat of the BMW, staring out the window as they drove to the trailhead. The collie had gotten into the car and settled down without incident, but Bryce still worried that he'd take off once the car door was opened. If last night was any indication, there wasn't much chance that Shep would come back if Bryce ordered him to, and Melanie would never forgive him if he lost her dog. Then again, she knew Shep better than Bryce did, and if he was the good heeler Melanie said he was, it shouldn't be a problem. If he wasn't, well, there were other ways to show a dog who was in charge.

The turnoff for the departure point was up ahead. As the car pulled into a parking spot, Shep seemed almost indifferent, his growling defiance of the night before replaced by a sullen acceptance of his fate. When Bryce opened his door, the collie slunk out of the car like a condemned man on his way to the gallows.

"Oh, come on," Bryce said. "It's not that bad."

There was a trail map by the parking lot; Bryce took a picture of it before starting out. It had been a long time since he'd hiked around there and the surrounding area was densely forested. He wanted to make sure he could find his way back if they got turned around. In spite of the grey skies, though, there'd been no rain that morning and the trail looked firm and dry. After a brief warm-up, the two of them headed out.

They started off at a sedate walk, Shep's displeasure showing in his limp tail and sagging shoulders. Bryce, however, refused to try to coax the border collie into a livelier mood the way Melanie probably would have. The dog would warm up to him in his own time, Bryce thought. In the meantime, Shep needed to follow his lead, not the other way around. He'd never known a dog

94

who didn't enjoy a walk in the fresh air, and at their present pace there wasn't much chance that the collie would give him the slip.

At least Bryce could enjoy the scenery. Benton County in the fall was a beautiful place, the last reds and golds of the maple trees giving way to the deep blue-green of the Douglas fir. The area around the trailhead had reverted to meadowland after repeated clear-cuts, and horned larks and red-winged blackbirds were singing their last songs of the season. As he and Shep continued their amble, memories of Bryce's visits to the area came back to him.

Up ahead, there was a wooded area where the trail descended, following a branch of the Luckiamute River. From there, it was just a little farther upstream that he and Melanie had gone kayaking for the first time. Her parents had taught her how to navigate the river at a young age and he'd been impressed by the ease with which she skirted the hidden hazards, her paddle barely riffling the water as it propelled her forward. Lying by her side as they dried out on the riverbank afterward, Bryce knew he'd met the woman he wanted to marry.

He and Shep were almost halfway across the meadow and the collie was starting to perk up. As their pace quickened, the sun came out from behind the clouds. It seemed like a good omen. Maybe, Bryce thought, the dog was finally warming up to him.

They were approaching the forest and Bryce could hear water rushing up ahead. As the grasses gave way to shrubs and saplings, the collie's speed continued to increase. What had begun as a listless stroll had gradually become a brisk walk and then an easy lope. Was Shep trying to make a break for it, or was this some sort of contest, a way to show Bryce who the alpha dog was?

If that was the intention, he thought, then Shep was in for a rude awakening. Since his law school days, Bryce had offset his long hours at a desk by running, competing in 5Ks and the annual Hood to Coast run — even a border collie would find it hard to outrun him. As their pace kicked up another notch, the two of them remained neck and neck. Bryce grinned.

Bring it on, buddy.

By the time they entered the forest, there was no longer any question about Shep's intentions. Panting hard, the dog kept glancing over at Bryce as if wondering when he would drop back. Instead, Bryce upped the ante, nearly passing the collie before the trail became too narrow for the two of them to continue side by side.

Suddenly, the broad, gently sloping trail they'd started out on became a treacherous footpath that rose and fell as it wove through the trees. Sweat dripped into Bryce's eyes, and when a low branch almost knocked him down he was grateful that Melanie had advised him to take her dog out without a lead. At that speed, on that trail, being tethered to an animal would have been suicide.

The increasingly hazardous path was forcing him to slow down, but Shep had also slackened his pace. Freed from the worry that the dog would get away, Bryce could catch his second wind, and as they continued their descent toward the river he settled into the rhythm of the run. Scenery passed in a blur as the wind whipped through his hair, but in spite of the uneven ground, low branches, and an occasional fallen log, his feet always landed securely. Even Shep seemed to be losing himself in exhilaration. It felt as if the whole dynamic between the two of them was about to change.

There was a blind corner up ahead where the trail rounded a trio of close-packed firs. As Shep disappeared around the first tree, Bryce heard a yelp and the sound of something scrabbling in the undergrowth. He rushed forward and saw the dog tumbling toward the riverbank.

"Oh, my god. Hold on, Shep!"

He swerved off the trail and executed a controlled slide down the same route the hapless collie had taken. Shep was lying at the bottom of the embankment, breathing hard and struggling to stand. Bryce bent down and stroked the dog's head, trying to reassure him as he gently probed for any sign of an injury. It didn't seem that anything was broken.

"That was a close one," he said.

As Shep got up, Bryce recoiled. The fur on the dog's side was saturated with a mixture of mud and decayed vegetation that was stomach turning. At least he was okay, Bryce told himself, trying not to think about what the stuff would do to his car. Maybe there was something in the trunk that he could use to cover the seat.

"Come on, boy," he said, trying not to breathe through his nose. "Let's get you back to Mama."

But as Shep took a step, he yelped again and stumbled.

"What's wrong?"

Bryce shook his head, feeling foolish. Of course the dog couldn't tell him what the problem was. Why even ask?

He sat back on his haunches, considering the possibilities. There was no blood on the collie's legs or paws, but the muck on his side made it impossible to tell if there was any on his side. Clearly, there was something wrong. Could it be a sprain? A dislocation? It might be as simple as a muscle cramp or as serious as a break — Bryce had no way of knowing. The important thing was to get Shep to someone who could help. He took out his cell phone and groaned: no signal.

They must be in a dead zone. Bryce wished he'd noticed when he took that picture. He glanced back up along the trail. How far were they from the top? A hundred yards, maybe two? They hadn't been in the forest that long, but the two of them had been running pretty hard. He looked down at the soggy, smelly dog and wondered which was worse: having to carry a forty-pound animal that far or trying not to gag while he did it? Bryce took a stick and tried to wipe away the worst of the slimy, sticky muck, but it was no use. Spreading it around was only increasing the stench.

Oh, well. Might as well get it over with.

"Come on," he said, scooping Shep into his arms. "Let's go."

Carrying an injured animal is not as easy as carrying a human being — even when it weighs less than half as much. A person can hold on, helping to lighten the load, and someone who's unconscious can be carried over the shoulder. An animal, though, is nothing but deadweight, and by the time Bryce got Shep to the top of the ravine his biceps were on fire.

"Here you go," he said, setting the collie down. "Let's see if you can walk now."

Shep struggled forward a few steps and collapsed in a heap, whimpering.

"That's okay," Bryce said, trying to catch his breath. "Just stay there while I call for help."

He took out his phone and walked several yards in every direction, checking for a signal — still nothing. Bryce sighed as he put the phone back in his pocket. He'd just have to carry the dog the rest of the way.

The level ground made the going easier, but Shep's injury had apparently become more uncomfortable and Bryce had to stop and readjust his hold several times when the dog began to whimper and squirm. By the time they got back to the car, Bryce was exhausted and his shirt was soaked through with the filth from Shep's coat. As he opened the car door and set the dog inside, Bryce tried not to think about what all that crap was doing to the BMW's interior. He stripped off his shirt and threw it in the trunk.

"All right," he said as he shut the door. "Let's get you home."

Melanie was standing outside the coffee shop when they arrived. Bryce had finally gotten a signal on his phone, and she'd promised to alert the vet. The smell was so bad that Bryce had to drive with the windows down, and even with the heater on full blast, his teeth were beginning to chatter. She peered inside.

"What's that *smell*?" She gasped and stepped away. "Oh, my god. Look at your car!"

"It's all right," he said as he rolled up the windows. "I set him on a couple of reusable grocery bags I had in the trunk. The worst of it is pretty much confined to the place where he's been lying."

"Poor Shep," she said, opening the back door. "Did you get an owie?"

Hearing her voice, Shep struggled to his feet and began shaking himself off. As stinking muck flew everywhere, Bryce covered his head and threw himself out of the car. Melanie stood on the sidewalk, screaming.

"No no! Stop, Shep, stop! Oh, Bryce, I'm so sorry."

Bryce stood on wobbly legs and leaned against his car. The interior was peppered with gobs of filth, the windows nearly opaque. He'd have to find an auto detailer. No way was he driving it anywhere like it was. Nevertheless, he told himself, if it meant that he and Shep had formed a bond, then perhaps it was worth it.

All in a good cause.

Melanie had taken Shep out of the back seat and was checking him over. As Bryce stepped around the back bumper, she gave him a puzzled look.

"I thought you said he was injured."

"He is," he said. "I had to carry him all the way back to the car."

"Well, whatever it was, he's fine now."

Astonished, Bryce hurried over to the sidewalk. The dog who'd been too lame to walk just minutes ago was leaping and prancing like a dervish. Other than the slick of foul-smelling mud on his side, in fact, there was no sign that anything was wrong.

"That's great," Bryce said through gritted teeth. "I'm so glad he's all right."

As Shep glanced over at him, Bryce could have sworn the dog was laughing.

CHAPTER 8

Melanie took Shep home and gave him a bath. As she set him in the tub and turned on the warm water, she almost wished that her collie didn't enjoy bathtime so much; after what he'd put Bryce through, she sort of felt that Shep deserved to be punished.

Poor Bryce. He'd actually been pretty good about the whole thing, but he and his car were a mess. Luckily, Walt Gunderson's nephew, Pete, had experience detailing cars and he'd been happy to come over and drive it back to his shop. Cold, damp, and without his shirt, Bryce had been in danger of hypothermia and Melanie insisted he take her car back to the inn. She and Shep had walked home, leaving a trail of stink in their wake.

While the first tubful of murky water drained, Melanie poured out a handful of coconut shampoo and worked it into the collie's coat, carefully running her hands along his sides and down his legs, still searching for any sign of an injury. Not only couldn't she find anything, but Shep didn't even flinch as she made her inspection. There was no way he'd needed Bryce to carry him. It made her wonder what was going on.

Shep hadn't greeted Bryce either of the times he was at the shop, and he wasn't very friendly when Bryce came to the house, either. Might her dog's behavior be a reflection of her own ambivalence?

Seeing Bryce again had reminded her of how much she still cared for him, and the contrast between their financial situations was sobering. It wasn't as if money was everything, of course, but being faced with such a stark reminder of how far she'd fallen behind in the last four years had sent her into another spiral of self-doubt. Perhaps Shep was just acting on feelings that she'd been trying to hide. Well, if that was the case, she thought, then the only way to fix things was to be honest about how she felt and get over it.

Melanie had hosed Shep off before bringing him in the house, but it still took three tubs full of water to get his coat clean. By the time the shivering, bedraggled collie got out of the tub, bathtime had clearly lost its charms. She threw a towel over his back and gave him a rubdown.

"Serves you right," she said. "Maybe next time you'll watch where you're going."

Half an hour later, Shep's coat was dry and the stench of rot had been replaced by a tropical bouquet. Melanie tied a bandanna around his neck and gave him a kiss.

"My, what a handsome boy you are."

The sun was out and she still had the afternoon covered. With so little time left until the election, she thought, it would be a shame not to get out and canvass voters, like they'd planned. Melanie decided to give Bryce a call and see if he was up for it.

"Hey, it's me," she said when he picked up. "How're you doing?"

"Better. Clean, at least."

"Yeah, it took a while, but Shep finally looks like himself again."

Melanie straightened the dog's bandanna.

"So," she said. "Are you ready to hit the hustings?"

"The *hustings*?" He laughed. "Since when did you become an old hand at politics?"

"It's something Walt said; I had to look it up. Anyway, there's a few hours of daylight left. You still up for some canvassing?"

"I'm pretty beat," Bryce said. "But sure. Why don't I swing by and pick you up in, say, fifteen minutes?"

"Great! We'll be ready and waiting."

As she hung up, Melanie gave Shep a stern look.

"All right," she said. "Bryce is going to come with us and I want *you* to mind your manners."

Melanie was at the window when Bryce pulled up to the house. She and Shep stepped out onto the porch and he waited patiently while she locked the door. When they got to the car, she opened the back door, put him inside, and slid into the front seat. Bryce opened his mouth and she held up a hand to stop him.

"Hold on a second," she said. "*Someone* wants you to know how sorry he is."

Melanie looked back at her dog.

"Aren't you, Shep?"

The collie hung his head, looking pitiful.

Bryce nodded.

"That's okay. No hard feelings."

"Okay," she told the collie. "Lie down now and be good."

Melanie snapped her seat belt buckle.

"There's not a scratch on him," she muttered. "He must have thought you were playing a game of some sort. Anyway, I'm sorry."

"Don't worry about it. Like I said, it's all right."

She nodded.

"Thanks for taking us. I guess it could have waited, but I was afraid that if I didn't start now, I'd just keep putting it off."

"It's fine," he said. "I'm feeling better. And you're right: It's important to keep the momentum going."

Bryce put the car in gear and made a U-turn. Melanie looked around.

"So," she said. "What do we do first?"

"That's up to you. Did you bring your list of likely voters?"

She bit her lip, remembering the half-hearted attempt she'd made the night before.

"I haven't really finished it yet. I guess I thought we'd just head out and see how it goes."

"Do you have a script? Topics you want to discuss?"

She rolled her eyes.

"I don't need a *script*. We'll just stop by, let them see how adorable Shep is, and remind them why I suggested we have an election in the first place."

"Okay." Bryce gave her a skeptical shrug. "So, how do we go about doing that?"

"Why are you asking me? You're the one

in charge."

"Which means that I give the orders and you find a way to carry them out."

She crossed her arms.

"Who made that rule?"

"Every boss in the world." He winked at her. "Come on, what's the most efficient way to canvass everyone in Fossett?"

"Well . . . I guess we could start at one end of town and work our way across."

"Have you got a map?"

Melanie felt a twinge of irritation. Was he really going to make her do *everything*? What was the point of having him along if he wasn't going to help?

"Why don't we just get started and see how it goes?"

"Fair enough. Have you got something to take notes with?"

"Um . . ."

Bryce nodded.

"We'll stop at Fossett House first," he said. "I've got a legal pad in my room."

Fossett's north side was a rural patchwork of agricultural concerns. Technically, the area lay outside the city's boundaries, but people there considered themselves residents, and excluding them would cause hard feelings. Melanie had chosen the sparsely populated area as their starting point so she could work out any kinks in her approach before hitting the higher-density areas where news of any missteps might give their opponent an edge.

Their first stop was the old farmhouse that Paul and Flora Grieb had turned into a chicken retirement home. Wooden coops dotted the landscape and wire pens surrounding the property held a motley assortment of geriatric hens pecking earnestly at the ground. Arching over the narrow driveway was a wooden sign that said:

GALLINA CANSADA
Home of the Happy Hens

Bryce raised an eyebrow.

"Unless I'm forgetting my high school Spanish, *Cansada* means 'tired,' not 'happy.' "

"The hens are tired *and* happy," Melanie said as she opened her door. "Tired of laying eggs and happy they're not on the menu."

She got Shep out of the back seat and felt an unaccustomed flutter in her stomach. It was one thing to talk about canvassing, she realized, but quite another to actually ask someone face-to-face for their vote.

"Flora *loves* my dog," she said, trying to banish her nerves with bravado. "I'll bet we get a donation here."

As advertised, the border collie was welcomed with open arms and the three of them were ushered into the sitting room like royalty. Flora had a smudge of flour on her nose and an apron over her blue calico dress. The house smelled of cinnamon and apple.

"Baking pies today, Flora?" Melanie looked at Bryce. "Her apple pies are to die for."

"Oh yes," she said, wiping her hands on her apron. "The women's club is having a bake sale."

She gave the collie a pat on the head.

"Would Shep like a little treat? I've got some of those bacon things left over from Halloween."

"I'm sure he'd love one."

As the older woman tottered off to the kitchen, Melanie and Bryce walked over to the couch.

"I told you," she whispered. "We're in like Flynn."

She sat down and clenched her hands to keep them from shaking.

"You okay?" Bryce said.

She nodded. "Just nerves."

Flora came back and gave Shep his treat.

"Sorry Paul isn't here," she said. "We heard a coyote last night. He's out counting the chickens."

"Wow," Melanie said. "A counting coyote. Who knew?"

Flora was in the dining room, retrieving another chair. She paused, looking nonplussed.

"What? A counting coyote? Wherever did you hear about that?"

"No, it was just that you said you heard one and —" She sighed. "Never mind."

So much for winging it.

Flora brought the chair in and sat down, carefully tucking the dress around her exposed knees.

"I suppose you're here to talk about the election."

"That's right, we are."

"Oh, my. This is very exciting. Things are usually so quiet around here, and now we've had *two* candidates show up in one day."

"Two?"

"Oh yes. Rod Blakely stopped by around noon and Paul insisted he stay for lunch." Flora simpered. "That's why I wanted to give Shep a little something."

Melanie's smile faltered. Had Rod already canvassed everyone in town? she wondered.

Suddenly, it looked like the Griebs' shoo-in votes might be in play. As the seconds ticked by, she realized how poorly prepared she was. She literally had no idea what to do or say.

Bryce leaned forward confidentially.

"Do you know, Flora, that bacon treat is the *first* contribution Shep has gotten to his campaign?"

Melanie stared. What was he doing?

"A contribution?" Flora looked flustered. "Well, yes . . . I suppose it was. The first, you say?"

"The very first." His smile was warm. "I really admire a woman who knows what she wants."

She reached up and patted her hair.

"Well, Shep's always been a good dog. I think he'd be a good mayor, too."

Melanie's eyes narrowed. Was Flora *blushing*?

"I agree. And I'll bet that if Shep could talk, he'd tell you how proud he is that he can count on your vote."

"Oh. Well, yes." She lifted her chin. "Of course he can."

Bryce turned toward Melanie.

"You hear that, Mel? Sounds like Flora has already made up her mind."

He stood and the other two followed suit.

"Well, we'd better let you get back to your pies. I plan to be the first in line at that bake sale."

Bryce took the older woman's hand in both of his.

"Thank you so much for your support."

"What was *that*?" Melanie hissed as they walked back to the car.

"That," Bryce muttered, "is called salvaging a bad situation. It's something lawyers get a lot of practice doing."

He opened the car door and Melanie put Shep inside.

"It's also the reason why you should have had a plan before you walked in there."

"Come on," she said, attaching the dog's harness. "How was I to know that Rod had been here first? Besides, you were practically seducing that poor woman."

Melanie imitated Bryce's rich baritone.

" 'I really admire a woman who knows what she wants.' "

He smirked.

"Just playing to the jury, sweetheart."

Melanie got into the car and made a note on the legal pad. *Flora Grieb: yes. Donation received: 1 bacon-flavored dog treat. Paul Grieb: ?*

The next three houses were a bust. At the mention of Shep's candidacy, the three of them were quickly turned away. No one seemed interested in Melanie's plan to make her dog the mayor, but then no one said anything about Rod Blakely, either. As they started off again, she checked the tally on her legal pad. Out of four homes canvassed so far, they'd gotten one firm yes, one firm no, and six question marks.

Bryce was still standing outside his open door. Melanie leaned across the front seat and looked up at him.

"What's wrong?"

"Are there beehives around here?"

"Why? Are you allergic?"

"To hornets, yeah. Not to bees." He shook his head. "I keep hearing a buzzing noise."

Bryce flinched as a shadow passed overhead.

"What was that?"

Melanie peered through the windshield at a black quadcopter hovering nearby.

"Oh, that's Les and Sal's drone. I'll bet that's what you heard."

She stepped out of the car and waved at it.

"They use it to keep an eye on their marijuana farm. They're probably wondering whether they should sic their dogs on us."

"What?"

"Don't worry about it," she said, continuing to wave. "They'll recognize my car."

At Les and Sal's, they were lectured on the futility of the election process, handed two homemade brownies, and ushered back out the door.

"I tossed them into the bushes," Bryce said as he got back into the car. "Think they'll notice?"

"That depends." She looked around. "Where's the drone?"

"I waited until it was out of sight." He started the engine. "Maybe the coyote will eat them and leave the hens alone."

"No," she said. "If the coyote eats them, he'll just get the munchies for chicken wings."

On her legal pad, Melanie wrote: *Sally Jennings: probably not. Leslie Jennings: ?* Donations so far were one bacon-flavored dog treat (eaten) and two pot brownies (left in bushes). It was starting to feel like the entire afternoon had been a waste of time.

She looked at Bryce.

"This isn't going very well, is it?"

He shrugged.

"I told you, canvassing is hard work."

"I know, but it's taking forever." She checked her watch. "It's almost six already and we've barely talked to anyone."

"That's because we started late, plus we're out in the boonies. Once we hit the residential areas, it'll go a lot faster."

"I don't know," she said, staring at the tally. "I still think we need to get some publicity if we're going to pull this thing off."

He shrugged and looked away.

"I don't know. Maybe," he said. "But we'll need to find someone we can trust. There are a lot of slimy characters out there ready to take advantage."

Melanie tapped the legal pad. They'd had the same argument earlier that morning. She understood the importance of getting out and talking to the voters, but what was wrong with finding someone else to help them drum up a little enthusiasm? Especially now that they knew Rod Blakely was covering the same ground they were.

"Surely, some of them are legit. I mean, I never would have come up with this plan if I hadn't seen that story on TV."

Bryce took a deep breath.

"Tell you what. My friend Dave Giusti is the entertainment editor at the *Gazette*. Why don't I give him a call and see if he can send someone out to do an interview with you and Shep?"

"You think they would?"

"All I can do is ask."

She thought about that for a moment. An interview in the paper wouldn't generate as much excitement as one on television, but it'd reach the people most likely to actually move there. It would also be a lot easier to get someone they already knew interested in Shep's story.

"All right," she said. "Sounds good."

"But that doesn't mean you get to slack off."

"Absolutely," she said. "No slacking. Got it."

Melanie felt her stomach growl. She'd been so nervous that she'd hardly eaten since breakfast.

"Listen, are you hungry?"

"Starved. Why? What have you got in mind?"

She grinned.

"You like bar food?"

CHAPTER 9

The Leaky Faucet Saloon was the oldest business in one of the oldest buildings in Fossett. Built by and for lumbermen, it was made entirely of wood, from the cedar siding to the oak floors, maple tables, and Douglas fir paneling inside. It was also a popular place for dinner.

Melanie grabbed a couple of menus from a stack by the door and Bryce followed her to the last available table — a wobbly two-seater just outside of the bathrooms. Heads turned as they crossed the room, no one bothering to hide their curiosity. Shep waited until Melanie had taken her seat, then lay down as far away from Bryce as he could, carefully tucking in his tail lest it be trod upon by anyone using the facilities.

Bryce sat down and Melanie handed him a menu.

"Was this place here before? I don't remember it."

118

"It was, but the building had been condemned back in the eighties. When we decided to revitalize the town, it was one of our first projects."

"I'm glad you did," he said. "It's a real piece of Americana."

A skinny waitress in jeans and a Grateful Dead tank top sauntered over.

Melanie smiled.

"Hey, Ashley. How's it going?"

"Fine. Busy."

She paused to push a wad of gum to the side of her mouth.

"What can I get you?"

"A bottle of Dos Equis, please. Shep will have his usual."

Bryce leaned forward.

"His *usual*? You're not seriously thinking of giving this dog alcohol, are you?"

"Why not?" she said, winking at Ashley. "It's after five, isn't it?"

Seeing the look on his face, the two women laughed.

"I'm kidding. It's just water. They keep a bowl for him in back."

Bryce set his menu aside and looked up at Ashley.

"What have you got on tap?"

She liberated her gum from its hiding place and gave it a couple of chews.

"On tap? Let's see." She frowned thoughtfully. "On tap, we've got beer."

"Oh. Well, in that case, I guess I'll have a bottle of Dos Equis."

"Good choice."

She turned on her heel and walked back to the bar.

He looked at Melanie.

"I don't even remember the last time I was in a bar that didn't have more than one beer on tap."

She shrugged.

"Welcome to the real world."

Ashley returned with their beers and set a bowl of water on the floor for Shep.

"You two ready to order?"

Melanie nodded.

"I'll have a bowl of chili — no onions." She smiled at Bryce. "You're welcome."

Bryce picked up his menu and glanced at it quickly. There hadn't really been time to look it over.

"I don't know. I guess I'll have the, um . . . Leaky Faucet burger." He snapped it shut. "Hold the mayo."

Ashley stopped chewing.

"That's the house special."

"I know," he said. "Does it come with cheese?"

"Among other things." Her gaze shifted to

Melanie and back. "Are you sure?"

Bryce felt a prick of irritation. Surely, even a place with only one beer on tap could make something as simple as a hamburger. He wondered if this was some sort of test, a way to mess with the stranger in town.

"I'm sure."

She pulled a face.

"Ooooookay."

"Also, I'd like to substitute a salad for the fries."

"You want a *salad*?"

"Please." He felt his lips tighten. "What kind of dressing do you have?"

She scratched her head with the pencil.

"Blue cheese and, uh, Thousand Island, I think."

"I'll have the blue cheese."

Ashley made a note on her pad.

"Is that it?"

"Yes."

"Okay. One chili, hold the onions, and one" — she looked at Bryce — "house special burger. Anything for the dog?"

Melanie shook her head.

"Shep's fine, thanks."

"It's gonna be twenty, twenty-five minutes. In the meantime, let me know if you need refills on those drinks."

She stuck the pencil behind her ear and

walked back to the bar.

"What is this," Bryce said as he watched her go. " 'Mess with the New Guy Day'?"

"I just don't think they get a lot of orders for the special."

Ashley and the bartender were sharing a laugh.

"Don't worry about it," Melanie said. "Nobody's messing with you."

He nodded. Even if he was being jerked around, Bryce told himself, it wasn't worth getting worked up over. He took a sip of beer and tried to calm down.

"Blue cheese dressing. I didn't even know people ate that stuff anymore."

She looked at him.

"What's wrong with blue cheese dressing?"

"Everything: cheese, trans fat, preservatives. I have to watch it, Mel. I'm staring forty in the face."

"You're thirty-four. That's a long way from forty." She shook her head. "Geez, it's not like you're going to die tomorrow."

At the mention of death, Bryce felt an unwelcome spurt of adrenaline. There'd been nothing in the news that morning about Colton and he was sure Glen Wheatley would have called if the guy had been picked up. The thought that a killer was still somewhere out there, gunning for him, was unnerving.

"I'm surprised this place is so busy," he said. "The food must be good."

"It is," she said. "But then we don't have a whole lot of choices, either. Fossett's too small for a McDonald's."

Bryce felt the corner of his mouth tighten.

"Not more than one, anyway, huh?"

She looked away.

"No. Not more than one."

He took another sip of his beer. It was the closest he'd come to broaching the subject of their marriage, and he wasn't sure how far he could push things.

"I'm curious," he said. "After we divorced, why didn't you change your name?"

Melanie shrugged.

"Why? Does it bother you?"

"It just seems a little odd, that's all. We were only married a couple of years —"

"Twenty-six months, two weeks, and five days."

"I guess I thought you'd want to go back to your maiden name."

She finished her beer and set the bottle back on the table.

"Too much of a hassle," she said. "I'd have to change everything: driver's license, utility bills, credit card. I'm not even sure they'd reissue my college diploma."

"Yeah, I'll bet you use that a lot around here."

Melanie pursed her lips.

"Oh, come on," he said. "Don't get offended. Wouldn't it be nice to be doing something meaningful with your life, instead of pulling espresso shots?"

"I *am* doing something meaningful. The people around here need me."

"You're right. I'm sorry. Like I said, I was just curious."

Bryce looked away, feeling chastened. Had he misjudged things? Maybe Melanie wasn't as ready to change her mind about the two of them as he'd thought. The problem was, he wasn't good at beating around the bush. To him, Fossett's shortcomings seemed glaringly obvious. He'd thought that by pointing them out he could show Melanie what she was missing; instead, he'd put her on the defensive. Clearly, it was the people around there she was attached to, not just the town itself. If he was going to convince her to leave, he'd have to show her that he cared about their welfare as much as she did.

Ashley came by with a pitcher and refilled Shep's water bowl. Bryce ordered another beer and looked around.

"So, who are these people? Maybe if I knew who they were I'd be able to come up with some targeted strategies for the campaign."

Melanie gave him a doubtful look.

"I'm serious," he said. "Different people respond to different approaches."

"Oh, all right."

She started scanning the dimly lit room.

"Well, for starters, Ashley is Kayla's mother."

"Kayla your assistant?"

He turned and squinted at their waitress, now chatting with a customer across the room.

"I would have said maybe an older sister. She must have been pretty young when she had her."

"Sixteen. Not much to do in a small town. Teens find their own forms of entertainment."

"What about the dad?"

"He was a heavy equipment operator on a logging crew until he misjudged a slope and rolled the machine. It's just the two of them now."

Bryce cringed. "What a way to go."

She nodded.

"Not that uncommon, unfortunately. In case you hadn't heard, logging's the most dangerous job in America."

He tipped his bottle toward a large blond woman sitting near the door.

"Who's that?"

"Helena Haas. Believe it or not, she and Selma are twins."

Bryce did a double take. The manager of the B and B was a tiny woman with mousy brown hair, a sweet face, and a full, soft body. The woman across the room looked like a Valkyrie: Tall and muscular, she had a long, straight nose, prominent chin, and thin lips.

"What does she do?"

"Excavation: tractors, earthmovers, backhoes. Too bad there's not much call for it around here anymore."

He thought about that while he looked around for another likely candidate.

"What about that guy at the bar?"

"Which one?"

"All the way at the end: red T-shirt, jeans, braid halfway down his back."

"Oh, that's Lou Tsimiak." She shook her head. "He's kind of a sad case."

"Native American?"

She nodded. "According to Walt, he's one of the last of the Luckiamutes."

"Like the river."

"Right."

Bryce took a moment to study the man who sat hunkered over his drink. There must be something about him that didn't invite social interaction. Even with the rest of the place filled to capacity, the guy had a six-foot radius of empty space around him.

"So, what's his story?"

"He was in the war — some kind of sniper, I think. Rumor has it he hesitated when a woman approached his platoon and she blew herself up. He was injured; some of his buddies got killed."

"Probably a scout sniper platoon; that'd make him a Marine."

She gave him a quizzical look.

"Oh yeah. I forgot your dad was in the Navy. How are your folks these days?"

"They're fine. They still ask about you."

"Still living in Washington?"

He shook his head.

"They got sick of the cold and moved to Coronado with the rest of the ex-Navy snowbirds."

The front door opened and a man in a green parka and camo pants walked in.

"Oh no," Melanie said, sinking into her seat.

"What's wrong?"

She shook her head.

"It's Rod Blakely."

"The opposition?"

Bryce watched as the man advanced toward the bar. There didn't seem to be anything especially attractive or charismatic about him — the sort of things that might make him a formidable candidate. If anything, in fact, the other patrons seemed to make a point of avoiding eye contact when he approached. This, in spite of the fact that he was nodding and smiling in an effort to ingratiate himself.

"He doesn't seem like much of a threat," Bryce said. "What are you so worried about?"

"I'm not worried," she said. "I just don't want him to come over here. If he sees us, I guarantee you he'll walk over and try to start an argument. It's what he does."

"Well, don't let him. The best way to handle people like that is not to engage. If he wants to argue, just don't give him the chance."

"Fine," she said. "If he comes over here, I'll let you handle him."

A place had opened up at the bar and Rod took a seat as he waited for his beer. As soon as he had it in hand, he turned on his bar stool and began checking out the room. The second he spied the three of them, he got up and walked over.

"Well," he said. "If it isn't Miz MacDonald and her little dog Shep."

"Hey, Rod," Melanie said.

He gave her a smug look.

"I hear you've been out talking to the voters. Having any luck?"

"What do you care?"

"Oooh, touchy touchy. This your hotshot lawyer?"

She glanced at Bryce and nodded as if to say, *Your turn.*

"That's right," Bryce said. "And you are . . ."

"The man who's going to whip your client's ass."

"Well, that should be interesting."

"Oh, it'll be more than interesting. We don't need outsiders telling us who to vote for."

"I agree."

"Fancy lawyers with your fancy cars," he grumbled. "Always causing trouble."

"Can't argue with you there."

"Overpaid busybodies."

"That's a fair point."

Blakely paused. He seemed nonplussed.

"You know you're working for a dog, don't you?"

Bryce shrugged.

"Honestly? I've had worse clients."

"Yeah." Blakely chuckled. "I'll bet you have."

The man leaned in closer.

"Ever defend a murderer?"

"No, but I've prosecuted one."

"He get the death penalty?"

"No," Bryce said. "Unfortunately."

Blakely shook his head.

"Damn weak-kneed juries. An eye for an eye — that's the way it ought to be."

Bryce said nothing. Let the man make of it what he wanted. He'd met guys like Blakely before. Most of them just wanted someone to hear them out. It cost him nothing to oblige.

The man looked back at his empty bar stool.

"Well, can't stand here listening to you two all day," he said. "Some of us still have work to do."

"I understand," Bryce said. "Nice meeting you."

Blakely returned to the bar and Bryce turned to Melanie.

"You see? It's not that hard. I'm sure he's a nice guy, once you get used to him."

"You're kidding, right? The man's an ass."

"No, he just has a competitive conflict style. Not to be pedantic, Mel, but guys like that see everything in the world as a competition they can either win or lose. Arguing is the way they assert their dominance."

He glanced over at the bar where Rod had launched into another harangue with the bartender.

"See that?" he said. "He's arguing again already. If that bartender's smart, he'll just roll over and let him win: problem solved."

Melanie looked from Bryce to Rod and back again.

"Where do you come up with all that hogwash?"

"It's called being informed; you ought to try it sometime. I find that avoiding snap decisions keeps me from making embarrassing mistakes. It's really not that hard."

She glanced over his shoulder, trying to hide a smile.

"What?" he said. "You don't believe me?"

"No. It isn't that. It's just, um . . ."

"Here you go," Ashley said as his plate hit the table. "The house special burger. Bon appétit."

Bryce's mouth fell open when he saw the conglomeration of foodstuffs on his plate: two beef patties, each one sporting a top coat of American cheese, a thick slice of ham, bacon, bread-and-butter pickles, tomato, lettuce, onion rings, and a fried egg, all of it dripping with barbecue sauce and served on an oversized bun. Instead of toothpicks, a serrated dinner knife had been plunged through the top to keep the whole thing from falling apart. Tucked into its side was a pale wedge of iceberg lettuce, coated in blue cheese dressing.

Melanie was holding her sides, trying not to laugh.

"Why didn't you warn me?" he hissed.

"I thought you knew," she said. "Not to be pedantic or anything, but you really should read the menu before you order."

CHAPTER 10

It was almost nine o'clock by the time Melanie and Shep dropped Bryce off at the B and B and headed for home. He'd insisted that she take the car, but in truth it hadn't taken much persuading. The temperature had been falling for the last few hours. At that point, it was just barely above freezing.

As they drove up to the house, she realized she'd forgotten to leave any lights on. Her little house looked dark and forlorn amid its well-lit neighbors. She put the car in the garage and got Shep out of his harness. The second she let him in the door, the dog went to his bed and dropped like a deadweight. Between running off with Bryce that morning and canvassing in the afternoon, she thought, the poor guy must be pretty well spent.

As she switched the lights on in the living room, Melanie thought the house felt colder than usual. She checked the thermometer

133

— sixty-eight, same as always — and wondered if she was getting sick. There was an ache in her chest that hadn't been there that morning. She headed into the bathroom and checked her temperature. Ninety-eight point four: no problem there. Maybe it was just indigestion. Even without onions, chili sometimes didn't sit well with her. She took a couple of antacids and chuckled. At least she hadn't ordered the house special.

They'd had fun at the bar. Bryce was a good sport about the Leaky Faucet burger and she'd enjoyed sticking a few pins in his lawyerly ego — something he'd never have tolerated in the past. He'd even admitted — reluctantly — that having only one beer on tap wasn't the end of the world. Melanie smiled. Apparently, she thought, it wasn't just his appearance that had improved. It was funny what age and maturity could do, she thought. Too bad that didn't really change anything.

Not that she wasn't enjoying his company — she was — and Melanie didn't know what she'd have done if he hadn't put together that campaign strategy. Bryce didn't get discouraged as easily as she did, either. Even having a door slammed in his face didn't seem to faze him. If it hadn't been for him, she'd probably have blown the visit with Flora and gone home to cry. He'd saved her when she made a bad start at the Griebs', listened patiently while Les and Sal told him that lawyers were ruining the country, and even managed to cut short one of Rod Blakely's harangues. Nevertheless, after she and Bryce had spent a day together, it was clear that he'd come there with an agenda.

Of course, Bryce was too clever to come right out and say so, but the comment about doing something meaningful with her life had made it pretty obvious. Sooner or later, she knew, the hints would stop and the two of them would be right back where they'd been four years ago. Only this time, saying good-bye would be a whole lot harder than it was the first time.

It hadn't happened yet, though, and in the meantime there was still a lot for the two of them to do. As for what might or might not happen after that, Melanie told herself, she'd just have to be like Scarlett O'Hara and think about it tomorrow.

Or maybe the day after.

She took out the map of Fossett that she kept by the phone book and spread it out on the kitchen table, setting the legal pad with her tally on top. Then she marked the area they'd covered that day and the places they still had to go. Melanie shook her head. Seeing it like that made her realize how big the task was that lay ahead. How were they ever going to reach even half the people in Fossett in time?

She closed her eyes, trying hard not to feel discouraged. Bryce had warned her that this was the hard part, the one-to-one connection that would pay off at the voting booth, but that didn't make it any easier. Every time someone closed a door in her face without listening, she knew the fear of failure was going to start building until it overwhelmed her, and then where would she be? When she'd dreamed about having Shep as Fossett's mayor, it seemed that her plan couldn't fail. Now that dream seemed as insubstantial as a puff of smoke. And getting her dog elected was only the first part. After that, they'd still have to find some way of getting the word out. She couldn't do it. It was too much.

Whoa, girl, slow down!

Melanie took a deep breath, reminding herself that it was late and she'd had a long, hard day. The only thing she needed to do was make a plan for tomorrow and get some rest. As for publicity, Bryce's friend at the *Gazette* would surely be interested in giving them a boost. A story like Shep's was perfect for the newspaper's local news section and they were more likely to get people to make a move to Fossett from Corvallis than from someplace farther afield. Then maybe they could start looking for other outlets, someone at the local radio and TV stations. Bryce's concern about slimy characters seemed a little paranoid to her, but then being a lawyer, she supposed he tended to see the uglier side of things, and his advice so far had been good. For the time being, at least, she'd just have to trust him.

With the next day's plan marked on the map and a preliminary script to follow, Melanie decided to call it a night. She put on her pajamas and brushed her teeth, wondering how much she'd changed since the last time the two of them had seen each other. Had age and maturity made as much of a difference in her as it had in Bryce? The honest answer was probably no. Since their split, she'd even asked herself from time to time if staying in Fossett had simply been an excuse, a way to keep from growing up and accepting responsibility, but the truth was she had accepted responsibility. Not for herself, but for everyone around her.

Maybe that was why there'd been so little enthusiasm for her ideas in the past. After all, it was easier to sit back and wait for someone else to solve your problems than to face them squarely and figure them out yourself. The problem was, the collapse of the lumber industry had made people lose heart. Those who could had left for greener pastures; the rest just seemed to be treading water. That was why she'd come back and that was why she couldn't leave. Not yet, anyway. Not until she was sure that the people there would be all right.

Shep's license jangled as he rolled out of his dog bed and padded after her into the bedroom. It was good to have someone else in the house. Melanie had gotten him in the first place thinking that she'd be safer living alone if she had a dog, but she never imagined that he'd be so smart or such good company. There were times when she would swear that Shep understood every word she said.

She crawled into bed and pulled the covers up to her chin. The cold sheets made her shiver. Shep curled up at her feet and fell instantly asleep, but Melanie just lay there, staring at the ceiling. Yes, she thought, it was good to have a dog in the house, but there were times when she missed having another person around. Days when her bank balance was low or a customer had been rude and all she wanted was for someone to tell her it would be all right. Or when something really amazing happened and she wished there were someone at home who would take her out to dinner so they could celebrate her good fortune. And there were nights like this, too, when the bed was cold and the house was dark and she wished more than anything that she could reach out and feel a warm body beside her.

Melanie felt the ache in her chest intensify and sighed. She'd finally realized what her problem was. She wasn't sick, she thought; she was lonely.

Darn you, Bryce MacDonald.

CHAPTER 11

If there was anything Chad Chapman hated more than meetings with his producer, he couldn't think of it — not before noon, anyway. He'd been doing tequila shots until two that morning and the world was still a bit of a blur. Why did they have to do this so early, anyway? It wasn't as if someone else had booked the rent-by-the-hour meeting room that day. As Roxie continued to blather, he watched a fly crawl across the table and wondered how it would feel to crush it under his fingers.

"What do you mean it's not finished?" she bellowed. "We already sold that piece to The Learning Channel."

"Could This Be Chewbacca's Love Child? What kind of learning is that?"

"What's wrong with it? It had a great hook — everybody loves Star Wars — and you have to admit that kid is pretty hairy."

"It was a stupid story."

Chad swatted at the fly and missed.

"That's not what you said when you took the assignment."

"I was drunk when I took that assignment," he said. "I'm not responsible for things I say under the influence."

"Oh, good," she said brightly. "Then I'm sure you'll change your mind once you sober up."

Chad sat back. Why was he putting up with this crap, anyway? It wasn't as if working for this sleazy outfit was the way to fame and fortune. Life was so unfair.

He reached for the Starbucks that Roxie had brought him and took a sip.

"Hey! This isn't what I asked for."

"Well," she said. "Now you know how it feels."

Chad grabbed his hair with both hands and yanked, hoping the pain would clear his head.

"What do you want from me?!"

"I want you to finish your assignments," she said. "I want to see you do the kind of work you've done for us in the past."

She started counting the episodes off on her fingers.

"The Best Poker Player in Vegas Is a Chicken; Chow Mein Führer: Inside Hitler's Secret Cookbook —"

141

He nodded. "That was a good one."

"— *I Won the Lotto and Still Can't Get a Date.* You've got great instincts, Chad — maybe the best in this business — but you've got the work ethic of a sloth."

"Hey, sloths are cool," he pouted. "Don't be picking on sloths."

Roxie's face purpled.

"We are not talking about *sloths*! We're talking about your future! You are *this close*" — she held up a thumb and index finger, close together — "to being booted out the door. Either you do your work or you go find a producer who'll put up with your BS. And good luck with that."

Chad put down his pen and sat up straight, taking a moment to fix his hair. He would not sink to her level, he told himself. They both knew this was an empty threat; it was time he reminded her of that fact.

"What does Graeme say?"

Roxie sat down and reached for her coffee.

"Graeme's opinion is that you should be given another chance." She took a sip. "However, he made it clear that the final decision is *mine.*"

Yeah, right.

"The truth is," she continued, "I never thought that the Chewbacca story was all that great. Nevertheless, really good story ideas are hard to find and the competition is fierce. Eyeballs aren't as easy to grab as they once were."

"That's true."

They both knew he'd won the argument. Why be a sore winner?

She looked at him and shook her head.

"For the life of me, I don't know why people trust you, Chad, but they do, and as you know, that's the key to success in this business. We don't have a stable of preening, overpriced talent here; we don't make millions selling airtime; we sell prepackaged videos to the freak show that is the modern entertainment industry. If we have nothing to sell, we literally have no reason to exist."

"Which is why," he said, "I need for you to give me something better than Chew-freaking-bacca."

"I agree."

She set the cup aside and started sifting through the pages in front of her.

"I found another story that I think will be right up your alley. It's about a dog that's running for mayor."

Chad deflated. "Seriously?"

"Hear me out. The hook isn't about the dog so much as it is about the town he lives in. It's been on the skids for years and the gal who owns him thinks that a dog mayor will turn the place into a tourist mecca. Think *Field of Dreams* meets *Deliverance.*"

He started doodling on his notepad.

"Where is it?"

"Someplace in Oregon."

He looked up sharply.

"The scene of the crime?"

She shook her head.

"Not that close. It shouldn't be a problem."

"Mmm," he said. "Well, I suppose it's worth considering."

"No. Not just considering — doing. Graeme might be on your side, sweetie, but his patience is wearing thin." She gave him a sour smile. "You're an expensive guy to keep around."

Chad sighed dramatically.

"Is this about Angie what's-her-face? What's the problem now?"

"She's asked the court to set aside your arbitration agreement."

"Oh, please. She knew what she was getting into as soon as I walked through the door. It's like they say: You can't pick up one end of the stick without the other. Fame cuts both ways. You take the good with the bad."

"Any more aphorisms you want to hit me

with before we move on?"

He stuck out his tongue.

Roxie sighed and put her head in her hands.

"Chad, you're almost thirty years old — you're not a teenager, even if you act like one. Believe it or not, I'm not your enemy, I'm actually on your side, but this Butler thing is different. Even Graeme is worried."

Chad ground his teeth and looked away. The truth was, he might have taken a teensy step over the line in that case, but he doubted that Angela Butler knew that. As long as she remained safely in the dark, her case would end up just like the other ones had: no harm, no foul.

"I thought that's what we had lawyers for."

"It's still a huge pain in the ass," she said. "And attorneys are expensive. I wouldn't press my luck, if I were you."

Roxie gathered her things and gave him a significant look.

"Fine. I'll do it."

"Good," she said. "I'll tell Graeme that we're putting Chewbacca's love child on the back burner —"

"Please do."

"— while you look into this mayor dog story. The woman's name is Melanie Mac-Donald; I'll email you her contact info. Give her a call. Find out what the deal is with her dog and see if there's enough there to build a story around. Depending on the angle, I've got at least two outlets who'll buy it in a heartbeat, so let me know what she says. If it's good, I'll get Mick to shoot the video and put you both on the first plane out of here. Get the footage, edit it into something juicy, and all will be forgiven. Agreed?"

"Yes, yes. Don't get yer panties in a twist."

He stood up and stretched, yawning dramatically; there was no sense in letting her think she'd won. He had no way of knowing how upset Graeme really was, but as long as Roxie was his gatekeeper, he'd just have to play nice.

"By the way," he said. "What's the name of this darling little Oregon town?"

"Are you ready for this?" She smirked. "It's called Fossett."

Chad paused, waiting for the punch line, then burst out laughing.

"Oh, my god. It looks like my career really is going down the drain."

CHAPTER 12

When Melanie and Shep arrived at Fossett House the next morning, Bryce was just finishing breakfast: eggs, bacon, toast, orange juice, and another carafe of Ground Central's best. Nothing fancy, but aside from the Beavertails Selma had snuck into the bread basket, it was darned near perfect.

"Have a seat," Bryce said. "I'm almost done."

Shep crawled under the table as Melanie took a seat.

"So. What's the plan for today?"

"Glad you asked."

She took the map from her purse and spread it out on the table between them. Bryce leaned forward to take a better look.

"Whoa, what's this?"

"I thought about what you said, you know, about being better prepared. So, I spent some time last night dividing the town into roughly equal sections. I figure if we can cover one section a day, we'll have contacted everyone in Fossett before the vote on Saturday."

Bryce pointed to the two black X's on the east end of town.

"What are those for?"

Melanie pointed to the larger one.

"That's Lou Tsimiak's place; we won't be canvassing there."

"Is this the Indian at the bar?"

She nodded.

"You'll see it when we go by. Place looks like a haunted house. He built this big tower in the backyard where he sits all day, watching for 'enemies.' "

"So, what's the other one for?"

"Oh," she said. "That's just a reminder not to disturb Horrible Harry."

Bryce raised an eyebrow.

"Bad guy?"

"No, just a bad-tempered rooster. He spends most of his time roosting in Everett Stubbs's truck, which is generally parked right where that X is. Everett says he's the best security system in the world."

"Why not just lock the doors?"

She laughed.

"It's a long story. Suffice to say, this way Everett doesn't have to remember to take the key fob with him when he wants to go somewhere and Harry has a comfortable place to snooze. It's sort of a symbiotic relationship."

"Well, at least it's only one house and a truck," he said. "The rest looks pretty straightforward."

He ran a finger over the highlighted and numbered areas.

"You know, you might just have a future in community organizing."

"No, thanks," she said, refolding the map. "Once this election is over, I'm done."

Bryce finished his coffee and set his napkin aside.

"Sounds good," he said. "Let's go."

The sun was dazzling that morning, but the lack of cloud cover had forced the temperature into the mid-twenties overnight and it was still barely above freezing as they got into the car. Melanie let the engine idle while she put Shep into his harness.

"Looked like Selma finally fed you a decent breakfast," she said. "How was it?"

"Very good. Why?"

She closed Shep's door and slid into the front seat.

"I had to chew her out yesterday for not keeping the larder stocked. It's hard, I know, when the place isn't busy, but she needs to learn to think ahead. If all goes well, we'll be having a lot of visitors soon, and I don't want her feeding them all a bunch of Beavertails."

"Really?" Bryce said as they pulled away from the curb. "I think those things are great."

They were starting in the southeastern part of Fossett that day. Less a true neighborhood than a random collection of dwellings, the ramshackle houses looked as if they'd been built from construction site castoffs. Poorly clad children played outside, the abandoned appliances and rusted-out cars in their yards serving as jungle gyms. Melanie had put Bryce in charge of the tally that morning. As they got out of the car, she noticed the look on his face.

"Needless to say, this is the less prosperous part of town," she said. "This is what happens when a big employer leaves: All those unskilled jobs that paid a decent wage go, too."

He nodded grimly.

"Let's do this side of the street, then the other side on the way back," she said, shivering. "I'm afraid if I get back in the car before we're done, I won't get out again."

"Sounds good."

No one answered at the first four houses,

though shadows on the curtains seemed to indicate that someone was home. Melanie and Bryce shook their heads and kept going. There was no sense in making enemies badgering people.

"We have a fair number of Russian families here," she said. "They're hard workers, but most of the older ones don't speak much English. I think they might be reluctant to try and talk to strangers."

They turned up a dirt path toward the fifth house and Melanie knocked on the door.

"This is Nikita and Ogie Gulin's house," she said. "We might have better luck here."

She paused.

"I hear someone coming."

The door opened a few inches and a small woman in a babushka peered out.

"Hi, Ogie," Melanie said. "We're here to talk about the election. Do you have a minute?"

The old eyes crinkled.

"Yes. Shep is good dog. I will vote."

"You will? Oh, that's fantastic. What about Nik? Do you think he'll —"

The door closed again.

"Oh. Well." She looked at Bryce. "Looks like one yes and one undecided."

He marked it on the tally sheet and they

started off again.

Just as she'd hoped, the canvassing was going much faster that morning than it had the day before. Partly that was because the houses were closer together, but also because only about half of the residents would open their doors. The responses they did get, though, were pretty positive, and though Melanie couldn't bring herself to ask for donations, Bryce didn't argue. It was obvious the people there had nothing to offer, and most seemed so excited to be casting a vote for Shep that there didn't seem to be any need to encourage them further.

As he and Melanie got to the end of the street, Bryce grinned.

"Don't look now," he said. "But I think we've attracted an audience."

Melanie took a discreet glance over her shoulder. The raggedy children who'd been following them began to disperse, looking around in an exaggerated parody of hide-and-seek.

"Poor things," she whispered. "Not much to do around here. We're probably the most exciting thing they've seen in a while."

"Well, in that case," Bryce said, "I think the least we can do is give them a show."

He reached into his pockets and pulled out a few quarters.

"Mel," he said loudly. "I think you've got something in your ear."

"I do?" she said, batting at her face.

He frowned and gave her a meaningful look.

"Oh," she whispered. "I get it."

Melanie gave an enthusiastic nod.

"Yes! I think you're right! What could it be?"

"Here," he said. "Let me take a look."

One of the bolder urchins inched forward as Bryce stretched out his hand and cupped it behind Melanie's ear.

"Why, look at this," he said, holding up a shiny new quarter.

"My goodness," Melanie enthused as he handed her the coin. "I had no idea that was there. Thank you for finding it."

Several more children had drawn closer by then. A small hand reached up and tugged at Bryce's coat.

"Can you find one in my ear, too?"

"I'm not sure," he said, winking at Melanie. "Let me see."

Nine more quarters were quickly "rescued" from tiny ears, and as Bryce amazed the children with his legerdemain, those who'd already received a quarter asked if they could pet Shep. Melanie saw curtains parting in the houses around them and one or two adults appeared on their front stoops.

She nodded at the faces looking out from the windows.

"I think you may have charmed their parents, too."

"Think it'll help?"

"It might," she said.

"Just in time, too," Bryce said. "The cash machine has run dry."

As the three of them set out again, the children tagged along, begging for more magic tricks.

"You look like the Pied Piper," Melanie said. "Got any more tricks up your sleeve?"

"A few," he said. "Why don't you see if you can make any headway with their folks while I hunt for props?"

Melanie waved at a man standing in front of the next house.

"Hi there," she said. "I'm here to talk about the election."

Three hours after their arrival, Shep, Bryce, and Melanie finally got back in the car. The tally was thirty-one yes votes, seven undecided, and only one no. As they drove away, the children cheered and waved, beating tiny hands on Shep's window in an effort to give one more pat of support. Bryce's tricks had indeed worked magic, Melanie thought.

The street that had been all but shut against them when they arrived had turned into a real success.

Bryce was looking out the window.

"Do you ever worry that bringing in more people will make it harder for folks like that to get by? If rents go up, they'll be out on the streets."

She shook her head.

"The reason they're living like that is because they don't have jobs. Once we get more people to move here, we'll be able to attract an employer who can provide them."

"But Fossett doesn't have the infrastructure to add a lot of new people. You could just end up with a lot of traffic and noise. Are you sure it's worth it?"

Melanie felt her lips tighten. Did he think she hadn't thought about that? She'd spent the last four years wondering if trying to help her town had been the right thing to do, and now that she had a plan that might actually work, she didn't need anyone trying to undercut her confidence.

Of course, she thought, his question had nothing to do with whether or not her plan would work; it was just the next step in Bryce's effort to get her to change her mind about the two of them. Would there be challenges ahead? Of course, but that didn't mean she should simply give up and let Fossett fail. She'd made a plan and she was going to see it through.

"I'm not really worried about it," she said. "Those things will take care of themselves."

He shrugged.

"For their sake, I hope you're right."

They were almost to Main Street when Melanie saw a streak of brown and white go darting through the bushes.

"Oh no," she said, pulling to the side of the road.

Bryce looked around.

"What? What is it?"

She set the parking brake and opened the door.

"The Stubbses' goats got out again."

Melanie stepped out of the car and opened the back door.

"Come on, Shep," she said. "We've got work to do."

The collie had apparently seen them, too. He was already struggling to get out of his harness.

"What about me?" Bryce said. "Can I come?"

She shook her head.

"No, you follow us in the car. The Stubbs farm is just down around the corner to the left."

He got into the driver's seat as Shep leaped out of the car. Bryce turned up the heater and rolled down his window.

"Mind if I listen?"

"No, it's fine," she said, her attention already fixed on the errant animals. "But whatever you do, don't get too close and *don't* honk the horn."

"Because of the rooster?"

"No," she said. "Because they're fainting goats. If you scare them, they'll be lying all over the place."

Melanie turned and faced the immature goats gamboling across Main Street. They were in luck, she thought. Kids were easier to control than adult goats. Shep stood at attention by her side, waiting for the signal. She raised her arm.

"Away to me, Shep."

The border collie took off, circling around to the right. Not at a gallop, but briskly in a sort of semi-crouch, his head and shoulders low, his tail down with the tip turned upward.

"That's the outrun," Melanie whispered. "I've sent him to a point beyond the farthest member of the group. At this point, I don't want him getting too close."

She walked forward slowly, Bryce inching the car along beside her.

In response to Shep's approach, the goats — who until then had all been going their separate ways — began to draw closer to one another.

"See that?" she said. "They know there's safety in numbers. Once they stop running all over hell and gone, Shep will be able to move them as a group toward where he wants them. That's called the lift."

Bryce pointed.

"Look at the way he's staring at them."

"That's important," Melanie said. "All prey animals react instinctively to the sight of a predator. When Shep approaches them like that, he makes them think he's a wolf and they start banding together to fend off an attack."

"They're playing the odds," he said. "If Shep were a predator, they figure he wouldn't be able to kill them all."

She and Bryce were almost to the ranch now. Thankfully, the gate where the kids had gotten out was on the opposite side of the driveway from where Everett parked his truck.

"Here comes the drive," Melanie said. "This is the crucial part. If one of them balks now, they'll break like billiard balls."

She looked at Bryce.

"Stay here while I get ready to close the gate."

Shep had circled the goats into a more-or-less coherent group and was moving them slowly toward the gate where Melanie waited. The adult goats were watching from an adjacent pen and bleating a worried welcome. Encouraged by their parents, the kids began to run. When the last one stepped inside, Melanie latched the gate behind them and glanced down at the dog.

"That'll do, Shep."

Bryce got out of the car and went over to join them.

"That's it, just 'That'll do'? Doesn't he get a treat or something?"

"Oh no," Melanie said, patting the dog's side. " 'That'll do' is the response every herding dog lives for. It means he's a worthy member of the pack. I guarantee you, Shep would rather have that than all the dog treats in the world."

"Well, if he can't have a treat, can he at least have lunch?" Bryce said. "I'm starving."

CHAPTER 13

The sign outside Gunderson's store said:

If we don't have it, you don't need it!

Bryce looked at Melanie.

"Is that a promise or a threat?"

She laughed. "Probably a little of both. Come on."

The three of them headed inside and walked back to the deli counter, where they ordered ham and Swiss sandwiches on Mae's homemade rye bread, then scoured the aisles for snacks and drinks while the sandwiches were being made. Bryce snagged a bag of Doritos and a Coke and Melanie opted for an orange Nehi, two Red Delicious apples, and some Oreos, plus a small bag of kibble for Shep. Walt was waiting for them at the front counter.

"Hey, Bryce. Long time, no see."

"Good to see you, Walt. You're right. It's

been a while."

Melanie set their purchases on the counter.

"I think Shep needs a walk," she said. "Do you mind getting this? I can pay you back later."

"Don't worry about it," Bryce said. "You two go ahead. I'll meet you back at the car."

The store had been in the Gunderson family for generations and it looked as if their checkout process hadn't been upgraded in years. Bryce found himself tapping his foot as Walt carefully rang up each item, and realized that the go-go pace he was used to had reduced both his attention span and his patience. He took a deep breath, reminding himself that there was no hurry.

"I hear you've left the DA's office," Walt said, ringing up the second sandwich. "Working for a big law firm now."

"That's right."

"Sorry to hear it. Seems like all the good lawyers are leaving government service. Pretty soon, there'll be no one left to take down the bad guys."

Bryce had heard the argument before. He'd made it himself, in fact, not all that long ago.

"Oh, there are still plenty of good prosecutors around. The DA in Portland is one of the best."

"Yeah, but budgets are always tight when the public's footing the bill. Sometimes it feels like justice is for sale in this country."

He tucked the sandwiches into the bag, holding back the bag of chips.

"It was good of you to come down here and give Melanie a hand."

"It was no problem. I was happy to help."

Two apples went into the bag next, then the Oreos, kibble, and chips. Walt put the drinks in a separate keep-'em-cold bag and rang up the total.

Bryce took out his wallet.

"What do you think of the plan to make Shep the mayor?" he said. "Will it work?"

The older man stared at the open till.

"I don't know. The town's thinned out since the timber industry folded, and it's changed the nature of the place. In some ways, of course, it's worse. Without the good-paying jobs we once had, several retail shops have closed, and we're down to only one school now, too. Other things, though, are better: There's less drunkenness, for one thing, and less violence overall. Plus, without all that heavy equipment rumbling through town, the place is a lot quieter than it was. The lack of public services is hard, too, but when people know they have to rely on themselves, neighbors take time to check on one another. I'm not saying it's ideal. I'm just saying it hasn't all been bad, either."

Bryce considered that for a minute.

"It seems like there ought to be some way to keep what's good about Fossett while still improving its economic circumstances."

"I agree," Walt said. "But most of us don't have the determination and energy that Melanie has. As long as she's hell-bent on making the town what it once was, I'm not sure that's possible."

"Have you told her that?"

"Oh, sure. More than once."

"But it didn't change things."

Walt shook his head.

"I've known Melanie since she was a baby and I love her like my own, but when she takes something into her head, she's as tenacious as a bulldog. I find it's better just to go along until she figures things out, one way or the other."

He gave Bryce a knowing look.

"You may have noticed the same thing."

He nodded. "A bit too late, unfortunately."

Walt counted out his change.

"Well, time goes by. Some things that were important don't seem so from a distance. I take it you haven't changed your mind about moving here?"

"I don't see how I can," Bryce said. "My job — no matter what you may think of it — requires that I stay in Portland."

"And you think you can convince her to join you?"

Bryce felt caught out by Walt's perceptiveness.

"I'd like to, yes. But like you, I'd rather she came to that decision herself."

The older man nodded.

"Well, whatever you do, be careful. I don't want to see either one of you get hurt again."

"Thanks," Bryce said, slipping the change into his pocket. "Believe me, neither do I."

They ate lunch in the car, neither one of them in the mood to sit outside in the cold. Melanie kept a collapsible dog bowl in the glove compartment; she poured out a measure of kibble for Shep and set it on the floor. He devoured it in seconds, then perched on the back seat, staring hopefully at their sandwiches.

Bryce ate quietly for several minutes. Walt's comment about his job had hit a nerve. Since leaving the DA's office, he'd had his own crisis of conscience. He was honest enough to admit that money had been the deciding factor in making the move to Norcross Daniels, but there were days when he felt as if he was walking a fine line between advocacy and collusion. Plus, there was still the whole Colton thing hanging over his head. Who knew how long it would be before that was resolved? He found himself dreading the day he'd have to return to work.

"You okay?" Melanie said.

"Hmm? Yeah, I'm fine. Just thinking about something Walt said."

"Anything you want to share?"

He shook his head.

"Sorry."

Bryce took another bite of his sandwich.

"This was a good choice. Thanks for suggesting it."

She smiled.

"You were a hit with those kids back there. I had no idea you knew all those magic tricks."

"What are you talking about? I practically wooed you with my magic tricks."

"Not rope tricks. You'd have been lucky to get a second date if I'd known about those."

He opened the bag of Doritos.

"Speaking of dating," he said, popping one into his mouth. "You seeing anyone these days?"

She gave him a look.

"Oh yeah. Can't you tell? I've got eligible bachelors falling all over me."

He covered his smile with a sip of Coke.

"You never know. They could be hiding in the bushes, ready to carry you off."

"Yeah, right." She started fishing around in the bag. "How about you?"

He took out another chip and shook his head.

"Too busy. Since the move to Norcross, I've been pretty much married to the job."

Melanie bit into an apple and chewed thoughtfully.

"What about Sofia What's-her-name? You ever go out with her?"

Bryce nearly choked on a Dorito.

"Who?" he croaked, smacking a fist against his chest.

"You know: dark brown hair, killer bod. She was two years ahead of you at law school. Man, did she have the hots for you."

He shook his head. The sting of spicy nacho cheese was making his eyes water.

"Oh, my god," Melanie said. "You did, didn't you?"

"I don't know what you're talking about," he wheezed, taking another swig of Coke.

"Well, if you didn't, then you missed out,"

she said. "Man, I was so jealous of her back then."

"Can we please change the subject?"

"Sure. What do you —"

Her phone buzzed.

"Hold on a sec," she said. "It's Kayla."

Bryce took another slug of Coke, relieved to be escaping the subject of Sofia Cardoza. It never occurred to him that she might have been interested in him back when they were in law school. He found the notion vaguely unsettling.

Melanie glanced at him and shook her head.

"No, of course," she said. "I understand. Yes. I'll be there as soon as I can."

She hung up and looked at Bryce.

"Helena fell and broke a tooth. Her husband's taking her to Corvallis to see a dentist, but there'll be no one to watch the shop this afternoon until she gets back."

She stuck the phone back in her pocket.

"I can't believe this. Just when we were starting to make some headway."

"It's okay," Bryce said. "Shep and I can manage alone."

Melanie gave him a skeptical look.

"After the outing you two had yesterday?"

"That was an accident — no big deal. Besides, it'll only be for a couple of hours."

"Well . . ."

He grinned.

"Either that, or I watch the shop while you take him."

She raised an eyebrow.

"Ever worked as a barista?"

"Nope."

"Never mind."

"Come on," Bryce said. "We've got the map. We'll be fine, right, Shep?"

Having given up his quest for a handout, the border collie was dozing on the back seat. He glanced from Bryce to Melanie and thumped his tail.

"You see that?" Bryce said. "He's totally cool with it."

"All right," she said doubtfully. "I guess it wouldn't hurt."

The two of them dropped Melanie off at Ground Central and headed to the next house on the map. In spite of his experience the day before, Bryce was eager to take Shep out again. So far, his plan to win Melanie over wasn't working as well as he'd intended; he hoped he'd have better luck with her dog. If he could prove to her that the two of them could get along, it would be that much easier to convince her that the three of them could live peacefully together

168

in Portland.

The next house on the map was in Fossett's historic district, only a few blocks from the B and B where Bryce was staying. Like Fossett House, it had been built in the Victorian style with dormers, exposed trusses, and Gothic windows. But whereas the B and B had been painted in muted tones of yellows and cream, this house was purple, with dark green shutters and bright yellow scrollwork running along the eaves. A gazing ball sat in the front yard and twin dream catchers dangled on either side of the porch. A brass nameplate on the door said: JEWELL DIVINE, PET PSYCHIC.

"Well, this should be interesting," Bryce said as he rang the bell.

Moments later, the door swept open and a slender woman in a gold turban and a velvet caftan opened the door. The interior of the house looked like two parts haunted house and one part *Hoarders.*

"Hello," Bryce said. "I'm Bryce MacDonald and this is Shep. He's running for mayor —"

Jewell gave them an enigmatic smile.

"I know. I've been expecting you."

She held her hands out to the dog.

"Shep, my dear. How are you?"

The collie stepped closer and she cupped

her hands around his head. Several seconds passed while she and the dog communed.

Bryce looked around.

"Right. Well, we, uh —"

"Sh-sh-sh." The psychic held up her hand. "Please don't interrupt."

He checked his watch, feeling like a fool standing there. How long was this going to take?

"He's running for mayor," he whispered.

"I know." Jewell frowned. "Be quiet, please."

Several awkward moments passed while Bryce cooled his heels. At last, the psychic let go of Shep and stood.

Not a moment too soon.

"So, the election is this Saturday," Bryce said. "Shep is really hoping he can count on your vote."

"Yes, of course," Jewell said absently, tapping her chin. "But I must warn you, there is a scandal in his past which you must deal with quickly or it will ruin his time in office."

Bryce nodded as if giving it some serious thought. He'd always made it a point not to argue with crazy people.

"Well, that's good to know, isn't it?" He looked at Shep. "Remember that. Honesty is the best policy."

Jewell was eyeing him critically.

"And he has a lesson for you," she said. "But Shep tells me you are a slow learner."

"Right. Aaaaanyway," Bryce said. "Thanks for the heads-up. I'll make sure we get that whole scandal thing cleared up right away."

Jewell folded her arms, looking pleased.

"Good. I look forward to the celebration."

As the two of them walked back out to the curb, Bryce glanced down at Shep.

"What do you mean I'm a slow learner?"

The next few houses were scattered among the numbered streets along the periphery of downtown. After the delay at Jewell's the two of them were once again making good time. For the most part, people were polite and enthusiastic about Shep's candidacy. Only a few mentioned being visited by Rod Blakely, and of those who did, no one had anything good to say about the experience. "The man can't take yes for an answer," was a common refrain. With only two houses to go, there were twenty yeses, five undecideds, and one firm no on the tally sheet and ten dollars (eight tired-looking singles, seven quarters, two dimes, and a nickel) and a Toll House cookie (delicious) in donations. Not a bad haul, Bryce thought. Melanie would be pleased.

Melanie would also be pleased, he

thought, about how well he and Shep had been getting along — surprising, really, considering how badly things had gone the day before. Maybe having Bryce carry him out of the woods had caused the dog to have a change of heart.

They'd come almost full circle by then. Melanie's car was little more than a block away. The sun was still out, but low enough in the sky that it barely skimmed the tops of the trees; he could feel the temperature dropping. At the thought of getting back inside the car, his pace quickened.

They were coming up on Lou Tsimiak's house. The place was even stranger in person than Melanie had described it. The yard was a hodgepodge of odds and ends that the man must have been collecting for years. Birdbaths, metal sculptures, and lawn trolls sat amid stacks of flat tires, broken lawn furniture, and two-liter bottles, filled with sand and half buried in the ground, all of it overgrown with weeds and wild blackberry. Whether it was PTSD or some other mental condition that had prompted this cache, Bryce was glad he didn't have to deal with it.

He felt a tug on the leash. Shep was trying to head toward the front door.

"No, no. We're not going in there," he said.

The collie glanced back over his shoulder, then tugged again.

"No," Bryce said, pulling firmly on the lead. "Not here. Come on."

Shep turned around, then sat down and stared at him defiantly.

"I don't believe this," Bryce muttered. "Shep," he said, giving the leash a tug. "Heel."

When the dog didn't budge, he tightened his grip and tried again.

"I said, *heel.*"

The collie stood, made a feint in his direction, and grabbed the lead in his mouth.

"What are you doing?" Bryce said. "Let go of that!"

Before he knew it, Shep had dug all four paws into the ground and started jerking on the lead, throwing his entire weight into the effort as Bryce held fast to the other end. The two of them were literally in a tug-of-war.

Bryce gritted his teeth. If Shep got away with this sort of bad behavior again, there was no chance that the two of them would ever be able to get along and any hope he had of convincing Melanie to move in with him would be gone.

Well, he thought, that wasn't going to happen. The collie was headstrong and spoiled and it was time he learned that he was not the one in charge.

"Drop it, Shep," he said, preparing for a final pull. "I said drop. *It!*"

And Shep did drop it. As Bryce put all his strength into one final yank of the lead, the collie stepped forward. With nothing to resist his backward motion, Bryce lost his balance and toppled into the bushes.

"What the hell was that all about?" he said, flailing his arms as he tried to right himself. "I swear, Shep, when we get back to the shop — Ow!"

He knew what had happened the second he felt it. Bryce swatted at his neck and got another sting for his trouble before the hornet flew off. He sat up and shook his head, feeling panic clutch at his chest. There was antivenom in the glove box of his own car, but he hadn't thought to put it in Melanie's and they were blocks away from Pete's garage. Even if he sprinted, he'd never get there in time.

He felt faint — his blood pressure was beginning to drop — and his tongue began to tingle. As his throat began to swell, he was finding it harder to breathe. Bryce began to feel an odd detachment from the world, realizing that he was about to die. Shep, too, must have known that something

was wrong, he thought. The collie was barking frantically.

Then everything went black.

CHAPTER 14

Bryce didn't know how long he'd been unconscious. For the first few minutes after coming to, in fact, he wasn't even sure he was alive. The last thing he could remember was standing outside and feeling at peace as darkness swallowed him. Who had found him and how he'd gotten there — wherever he was — was a mystery.

There was an ache in his thigh and his whole body was buzzing, as though a current of electricity had been plugged into his nervous system. Bryce thought he might have jumped out of his skin if it weren't for the heavy blanket that covered him, pressing down like a giant hand. He smelled incense burning. Somewhere in another room, a man was talking. He licked his lips, trying to relieve the parched feeling in his mouth, and lifted his head.

He was lying on a bed in the middle of a room he'd never seen before. On the nightstand next to him was a glass of water, a thermometer, and an odd-looking incense burner from which a wisp of fragrant smoke was rising. A small desk and chair on the opposite wall were the only other pieces of furniture. The rest of the room was filled with Native American artwork: a woodcut of a bald eagle soaring over treetops; masks that looked like bears, beavers, and wolves; a coat made out of feathers. Shelves on two of the walls held more treasures: tiny carved figures in native dress, pots woven from prairie grass, a peace pipe, and, incongruously, a small shadow box with six military service ribbons.

The conversation in the other room stopped and Bryce heard footsteps coming closer. He laid his head back down just as a barrel-chested man in a T-shirt and jeans walked in. The man had a broad, flat face and a square jaw that suggested belligerence, but the deep-set eyes were kind, with creases that fanned out across his cheekbones like wing feathers. His long black hair, shot through with wiry strands of white, reached well past his shoulders.

"So," he said. "You're awake."

"Yes, thanks to you. You're Lou Tsimiak."

"Yep, that's me."

"How did —"

Bryce coughed. His throat was so dry it was hard to talk.

"Here."

The man slid an arm under his back, lifted him gently, and held the glass of water to his lips. Bryce took a few grateful swallows and lay back on the bed.

"Thank you," he said. "How'd you find me?"

Tsimiak looked at him as if the answer were obvious.

"Wolf called me. I answered."

Bryce shook his head. Was this some sort of Indian thing?

"Wolf," the man said again, pointing at the floor.

He raised himself on one elbow and peered over the side of the bed. Shep was lying next to the bed, looking remorseful.

"When I brought you inside, Wolf came, too. He's been sitting vigil, waiting for you to wake up."

Bryce fell back against the pillow.

"Well, I suppose it's the least he could do, considering he nearly killed me."

He looked around at all the Indian paraphernalia.

"This is some collection you've got in here."

Tsimiak walked over to the desk and

removed a small box from the top drawer. He glanced at the artifacts and nodded curtly.

"It was my therapist's idea. After what happened over there . . ."

He shook his head.

"Didn't know who I was: a warrior or just the White Man's tool? She'd heard of a Chinook holy man who had good luck working with vets suffering from PTSD. I did the whole sweat lodge thing, grew my hair out — it felt like I was getting my spirituality back. These things you see here make me feel connected to all of that."

"So, did you find your answer?"

Tsimiak closed the drawer and took a few seconds to consider.

"Still working on it, I guess."

Bryce nodded toward the badge and service ribbons in the shadow box. As the son of a military man, he was familiar with their meanings: Afghan campaign, Global War on Terrorism Expeditionary Medal with a V for valorous conduct, Purple Heart, Bronze Star, a Distinguished Marksman Badge.

"Looks like you had a pretty distinguished military career."

Tsimiak shrugged.

"I did what I had to do."

"Sorry," Bryce said. "I didn't mean to bring up a sore subject."

The man turned and looked at him.

"Some Indians don't believe in military power. They think guys like me are being exploited by the government, but I don't feel that way. The Marines didn't make me a warrior; they just gave me a place to use the skills I already had. Now that I've mustered out, I still perform the rituals of a warrior — rise at dawn, say my prayers, maintain my weapons, exercise my mind and body — but a warrior without a war is just a man that other men fear. If I'm not a warrior, what am I here for?"

He sighed.

"Maybe when I find that answer, I'll be at peace."

Bryce turned his head and took a closer look at the incense burner. It was shaped like a man draped in buffalo robes, with two feathers in his hair. He held a pipe in one hand and his chin was held high. Smoke from the incense rose from his mouth.

"Who's this guy?"

"A Kiowa holy man. The smoke he exhales is supposed to have healing powers. After I went through the sweat lodge ceremony, I spent some time studying native healing."

"Did you use some kind of Native American medicine on me?"

Tsimiak nodded solemnly.

"It called EpiPen."

He laughed out loud.

"Just messing with you, dude. Sorry. A little Indian humor there."

Bryce chuckled.

"No, it's okay. I probably deserved that."

Tsimiak opened the box and set it on the nightstand.

"I'm gonna check your blood pressure while we wait for the doc to arrive."

He took Bryce's arm out from under the blanket and wrapped it in a cuff.

"Melanie tells me you're a Luckiamute. Is that true?"

"Depends on who you ask. You ask me, I say yes. You ask the tribes around here, they'd say no."

"Why's that?"

Tsimiak started pumping up the cuff.

"White women. Too many of my ancestors married them. Besides, the BIA folded the Luckiamute tribe into the Grande Ronde years ago."

"If you'll forgive me for saying so, you look like an Indian to me."

"Hey, no offense taken, man. Some people pay through the nose for this kind of bronze beauty." He lifted his chin and struck a pose. "Eat your heart out, paleface."

Bryce laughed. He was starting to like this guy.

"So, I guess there's no chance you'd be welcome on a reservation."

The man waved the thought away.

"Who needs 'em? My people lived right here for thousands of years before white men came. If I want to feel close to them, all I have to do is take a walk in the woods. Now that the loggers are gone, the land can finally recover. Soon, the trees and the animals who depend on them will return. No," he said. "This is where I belong; not running a craps table at some casino."

In spite of the man's flippant attitude, Bryce sensed there was real hurt there. It seemed to him that Lou Tsimiak was caught between two worlds.

The Indian checked his blood pressure reading and took off the cuff.

"Getting better," he said, stuffing it back into the box. "You still feel like you got ants crawling under your skin?"

Bryce nodded. "About a million of 'em."

"Yeah, adrenaline will do that to you — fight or flight. Beats dying, though."

A furry head poked up over the covers and Bryce felt Shep snuffling his exposed hand.

Tsimiak grinned.

"Looks like someone's sorry."

Bryce hesitated a second, still irked at the collie for dumping him into the bushes. Nevertheless, when he looked into the eyes staring pleadingly up at him, he couldn't resist.

"Oh, all right."

He stroked the dog's head and received a grateful lick in return.

"I guess I shouldn't be too angry," he said. "After all, you did call for help."

Tsimiak stood and stretched.

"You're gonna feel like crap for the next day or so. See if the doctor will give you something to help you sleep. Also, the place on your thigh where I injected you will be tender; you'll probably have a nasty bruise."

Bryce heard knocking on the front door downstairs. Tsimiak put the cuff away and smiled.

"Sounds like the cavalry's arrived."

CHAPTER 15

Melanie sat on the edge of the bed, watching Bryce with concern. She'd come home to see how he was doing and found him having another one of his "spells." The doctor had given him a sedative last night to help counteract the jumpiness and anxiety caused by the EpiPen, and within minutes of Melanie getting him to her house he'd fallen into an exhausted sleep. Not long afterward, though, he'd begun tossing his head and moaning as if engaged in some sort of struggle. As she sat there, watching him twitch and grimace, she almost wished she'd asked the doctor to give her something to relieve her own anxiety. What, she wondered, was going on behind those closed eyes?

The first time it happened, she'd called the doctor in a panic, sure that Bryce was having some sort of seizure, but he'd assured her that it was a normal, if somewhat uncommon, reaction. The sudden loss of blood pressure, followed by an equally sudden jolt of epinephrine, had been a shock to both his brain and body, and although the sedative made it possible for him to sleep, it couldn't counteract what he'd already endured. Whether these spells were the reflex reactions of an overstimulated nervous system or the physical manifestations of some mental trauma was unknowable at this point, he told her. The best thing to do was to keep Bryce quiet and comfortable.

Melanie reached out and laid a hand on his damp forehead. To check for a fever, she told herself, but what she was really seeking was reassurance. Try as she might, she couldn't keep from obsessing about what might have happened. What if Lou hadn't found him when he did, or hadn't had an injector on hand, or if Shep's barking hadn't alerted him that something was wrong? The thought that she might have lost Bryce forever made her feel sick at heart.

As the spell passed, beads of sweat began to form on Bryce's upper lip. With a guilty pang, Melanie realized she'd probably put too many covers on him. The doctor had warned her that his temperature might fluctuate until the epinephrine was out of his system, and she'd been anxious to get him warmed up quickly. Her little bungalow lacked the sort of modern insulation that newer houses had and when she and Lou had gotten Bryce into bed last night, there'd been a definite chill in the room. Perhaps, she thought, she'd overdone it a little.

Or maybe it's that big, hairy dog lying next to him.

"Back off a little, Shep," she said, giving him a shove. "Let Bryce cool off."

The collie retreated a few inches, then slowly began creeping back.

"Oh, never mind."

Melanie shook her head. From the moment Bryce had tumbled into the bushes until she tucked him into bed last night, the collie had refused to leave his side. Whatever had happened between the two of them, it had turned their relationship upside down.

She got up and started peeling the blankets off one by one. For the last few hours, she'd been fantasizing about what it would be like to have Bryce back in her life, the two of them living together, building a new life for themselves in Fossett. For a little while, she'd even convinced herself that Bryce could be happy living there, too, that he was ready to make the commitment he'd backed out of years before. Now, however, Melanie wondered if she was just being foolish. She'd seen this movie before and it didn't have a happy ending.

And yet . . .

And yet there was still a stubborn part of her that wanted to believe Bryce really had changed his mind. Why else would he have come there in person instead of simply calling her back? The reason he'd given — that he'd needed some fresh air — was patently false. And then there was all the work he'd done on Shep's election campaign. He had to know that once her dog was the mayor, Melanie would find it impossible to leave. Would Bryce really have put in that much effort if he didn't want Shep to win?

Then yesterday, Melanie had seen another side of Bryce — one she'd thought was gone forever — when he'd entertained those kids in the street. Yes, it had given her an opportunity to talk to their parents about the election, but it had shown her that he wasn't the stubborn, controlling person she'd been making him out to be. He was the patient, kind, and funny man she'd fallen in love with.

Of course, caring about Fossett's future wasn't the same as wanting to be a part of it, and if Shep did become the mayor, it would only be the first step in her plan to revitalize the town. The real question was whether or not Bryce would be willing to stay for the long haul. What if the position at Norcross Daniels was his dream job? Even if it wasn't, moving would be a big disruption: He'd have to sell his condo, find a place to live, look for another job. In spite of Bryce's claim that he had no personal life, there must be friends and colleagues he'd be sorry to part with, too, and after his reaction to Melanie's comment about Sofia Cardoza, the question of whether or not he was seeing anyone was still unanswered. Before she got too excited about the possibility of a reconciliation, Melanie needed to be sure that Bryce wouldn't be as unhappy with his choice as she would have been had the decision gone the other way.

Nevertheless, as she watched him lying on her bed with Shep snuggled close, Melanie couldn't keep herself from hoping he'd stick around.

With the extra blankets removed, Bryce started coming around. His eyelids began to flutter. He opened his eyes and smiled weakly.

"Hey."

"Hey yourself."

Melanie reached forward and brushed a few damp strands of hair from his forehead.

He lifted his head and tried to look around.

"How long have I . . . ?"

"Been out?"

She glanced at the clock.

"Well, let's see . . . Lou and I brought you here around six last night and it's twelve thirty now, so what's that? Eighteen, almost nineteen hours? You've had some lucid moments since then and I managed to get some soup into you last night, but for the most part you've been zonked."

Bryce let out a whoosh of air and shook his head.

"I'm sorry. The canvassing —"

"Is going fine." She chuckled. "No offense, but your accident is the best thing that's happened to the campaign. Volunteers have been coming by the shop all day, asking how they can help."

He licked his lips.

"That's great," he said. "I'm glad."

"Helena's helping Kayla at the shop so I could come see how you were doing."

Shep put his head back on Bryce's chest and he began petting the dog absently.

"I've been a little worried," she said. "You've been thrashing around a lot in your sleep. The doctor said it was nothing serious, but I couldn't help wondering if something was bothering you."

His gaze slipped away.

"Must have been a bad dream."

Melanie felt a flash of anger. She'd spent the last few hours thinking that things had changed and now here was the old Bryce, putting up a false front rather than telling her an uncomfortable truth. Well, she wasn't going to put up with it — not again. If there was a chance that they could work things out, then the truth telling had to start now, not in some imagined future.

"Bryce, do you love me?"

He seemed shocked for a moment; then his face softened.

"Of course I do. Always have."

"Well, I love you, too," she said, her voice thick. "But I'm not going to be lied to anymore. When you came into the shop on Saturday, you looked scared out of your wits. I wondered what was wrong, but I didn't say anything because, well, I didn't think I had the right to pry.

"But things have changed — at least I think they have — and I've been watching you writhe and thrash in this bed for half a day wondering what the hell was wrong. If you don't tell me right now, that's it. If we can't be honest with one another then let's just call it quits."

Bryce closed his eyes and sighed deeply. Melanie prodded his chest.

"Oh no. Don't you dare fall asleep again."

"I'm not," he said. "It's just something I've been trying not to think about."

"Well, judging from the way you've been tossing the covers around, I'd say you're doing a pretty crappy job of it."

He chuckled ruefully.

"You're right."

He glanced down at Shep and fingered a silky ear.

"Do you remember a guy named Jesse Lee Colton?"

Melanie felt a chill. Who in the Northwest didn't remember him? She'd read an article once that described the man's killing method as "vivisection." She nodded.

"You prosecuted that case, didn't you?"

"I did. At the sentencing, he promised to kill every one of us the same way."

She felt a frisson of fear.

"Oh, god. He hasn't escaped, has he?"

Bryce nodded.

"Last week. I ran into Glen Wheatley right after you called. He said I should make myself scarce until they found him."

Melanie looked away. So, Bryce's coming there had had nothing to do with starting over or moving to Fossett. He'd just been running away.

"That's why you came here."

Bryce reached for her hand.

"At first? Sure, that was part of it, but that's not why I stayed."

She nodded, trying to hold back tears. Why had she been so foolish?

"It's all right," she said. "The important thing is that you're safe."

Bryce was struggling to sit up.

"Will you cut it out? I told you, that's not the only reason I came. I wanted to see you again. I hoped —"

He shook his head and lay back on the pillow.

"Since I got here, things have been so good, you know? I didn't want to spoil it by telling you what was going on back there. I wasn't sure you'd understand."

Melanie smiled.

"All things considered, I'd say you were right to be concerned," she said. "I'm sorry. I guess I shouldn't have jumped to conclusions. Almost losing you has made me realize how much you still mean to me, but I'm still confused about where we go from here. I just don't know if it's enough."

He nodded in agreement.

"Yeah, me too."

"For the time being, maybe it's enough

that you're still alive and we both feel the same. We can figure out the rest later."

Melanie looked at her watch.

"Speaking of which, I'd better get back to the shop."

Bryce tried to sit up.

"Let me help."

"No, you don't." She pushed him gently back onto the pillow. "I just stopped by to see if you wanted some lunch."

Bryce shook his head.

"No thanks. I'm not hungry."

"Then in that case, I'm going to head back to work. Your phone's here by the bed if you need anything and Selma washed your clothes, so if you feel like getting dressed later, they're sitting on the dresser. For now, though, I think you need to just stay in bed and get some more rest."

She hesitated a moment, then leaned forward and gave him a kiss.

"I'll be back by five."

There was no one at the counter and only three tables occupied when Melanie got back to the shop. She thanked Helena for the help and insisted that Kayla take a break. With all the election stuff going on and now Bryce's illness, she'd been leaning on the girl pretty hard. She'd have to find some way of making it up to her.

"Everything go okay while I was gone?"

Kayla was sitting in the back room, checking her phone.

"Yeah. A few of the regulars came by and asked about Bryce. I told them you were at home checking up on him."

"How did Helena do?"

"Okay." The girl shrugged. "Mostly, she just cleaned stuff."

Kayla gave her a sly smile.

"So," she said. "Are you and Bryce getting back together?"

Melanie felt her face flush. She'd been trying not to talk too much about how her feelings had changed. Apparently, she hadn't been doing a very good job of it.

"I don't know," she said.

"Mom likes him. She had us all in stitches showing us what he looked like when she set the Leaky Faucet burger down on the table."

The girl opened her eyes and mouth like a cartoon character.

Melanie laughed.

"I suppose I should have warned him, but he took it well."

"He seems like a nice guy. I hope it works out."

"Yeah. I hope so, too."

She turned away and started emptying the dishwasher. After all the disruption of the last few days, it was calming just to have something simple and mindless to do. Melanie felt a smile tug at her lips as she thought about Bryce. She'd taken a risk forcing him to tell her about Colton's threat. The news had been so much worse than she'd imagined that she'd been almost sorry that she had, but she didn't doubt that it had been the right thing to do. Unless they stopped making the same mistakes that they had in the past, it made no sense to even try to have a future together.

Kayla put her phone away.

"Would you mind if I take a break? I'll only be a few minutes. Mom needs me to pick up a couple of things at Gunderson's for dinner."

"Sure, go ahead," Melanie said. "I'm fine."

The girl grabbed her jacket and slipped it on.

"Oh, I almost forgot."

She reached into her pocket and took out a slip of paper.

"Some guy called for you. Said he was interested in maybe interviewing you about Shep."

She held out the slightly crumpled note.

"Sorry. I was going to take it over to your

place if you didn't get back before I left."

"No problem."

As Kayla walked out, Melanie smoothed the wrinkles out of the paper and looked at the name and number on it. She frowned.

Chad Chapman.

The name sounded vaguely familiar, but she didn't recognize the area code. She shook her head. Bryce's warning about scam artists and her own natural skepticism made her wary of any unsolicited calls. Then again, she thought, what if the guy was legit? Bryce's friend Dave still hadn't called back. Maybe she'd hang on to it, just in case. Melanie folded the paper, slipped it into her apron pocket, and promptly forgot about it.

CHAPTER 16

Bryce had been sleeping off and on for the better part of the day before he finally got out of bed. He'd been only vaguely aware of Melanie's leaving that morning, but her visit around noon was still etched in his memory. In spite of his recent debility, he felt stronger, more optimistic about the future, than he had in years; even his recent victory at work paled in comparison. It felt as if he and Melanie were on the cusp of building a newer, more honest relationship.

Shep was stretched out on the bed beside him. When Bryce stirred, the collie lifted his head and thumped his tail in a cautious greeting. Bryce reached out and stroked the dog's head.

"You still here? I thought you'd be at work with Mel."

Shep wriggled forward and nuzzled his cheek.

"Aw, you weren't worried about me, were

you? You should know I'm not that easy to get rid of."

Bryce threw back the covers and sat up, feeling his head swim, then licked his lips with a sticky tongue; his mouth tasted like something had died in it. He walked into the bathroom, gargled a mouthful of water, spit it out, and drank three full glasses in rapid succession. When he was finished, he set the glass back down and stared at himself in the mirror.

His face was pale, his hair a tangled mess of greasy strands, his eyes a bit glassy. As bad as the hornet's sting had been, the aftermath had almost been worse: a dream — the same one, over and over — in which Jesse Lee Colton had appeared, blade in hand, his wild eyes glittering with excitement, poised to cut and stab and slice through his flesh. Bryce looked, he thought, exactly the way he felt: like a man who had just cheated death.

He heard his phone ring and immediately recognized the ringtone: it was his office. As Bryce walked back into the bedroom, he felt his stomach clench. No doubt, he'd be in some sort of trouble. When he took off on Friday night, he hadn't known how long he'd be gone; putting as much distance as possible between himself and Jesse Lee

Colton had been the only consideration. Now, he realized, he should have given his admin an ETA. Having to cover for his unexplained absence would no doubt have put her in an unforgiving mood. As he picked up, he was prepared for a tongue-lashing.

Gemma's voice was tense.

"Where are you?"

"Out-of-town emergency," he said. "I thought I'd be back by now or I would have called. Sorry."

He heard her deep intake of breath and hoped it wouldn't be the prelude to something worse.

"Well, you'd better get back here pronto," she said. "Daniels has called an all-hands for tomorrow morning at nine. Unless you're on death's doorstep, missing it isn't an option."

Bryce grumbled silently. He hated meetings on principle, but all-hands were the worst. The name lent them a sense of urgency that required everyone's attendance, but without an agenda, any actual crisis was impossible to prepare for. Most likely, this was just another chance for the senior partners to lord it over their underlings. Daniels, in particular, loved nothing more than to snap his fingers and watch everyone jump.

Nevertheless, whether this meeting would be fruitful or even necessary wasn't the point. Bryce was a professional; this was his job. As long as he was an employee of Norcross Daniels, he'd jump as high as they wanted him to. Even so, for a second Bryce was tempted to mention the hornet sting, but he decided not to chance it. His unexplained absence had already reduced the chances of being believed to zero.

"No problem," he said. "Thanks for letting me know."

As he put down the phone, a dozen tasks were fighting for Bryce's attention. There was no time for a haircut, but he'd definitely need to get his suit cleaned, or at least pressed, and his shoes would have to be shined. There must be dozens of emails in his in-box to answer, too, and angry clients to contact, all of which would have to be done before he got back. Once he set foot in the office, he'd be right back in the maelstrom with no time to catch up.

He dialed the garage to see if his car was ready.

"Sorry, man," Pete said. "I'm gonna need another day to finish it. You wouldn't believe where some of that crap ended up."

"No, I understand," he said, remembering

the spray of sludge when Shep shook himself off in the back seat. "Just give me a call when it's done."

Bryce set the phone down and pursed his lips. He knew Melanie would let him borrow her Honda, but he hated to ask, especially since his absence had already disrupted their campaign schedule. His only other option, though, would be renting a car in Corvallis, and giving him a ride out there would take up even more of her time. At this point, he didn't have much choice. He'd just have to take her at her word and make as quick a turnaround as he could.

First, however, he needed to take a shower. Melanie would be home soon and he didn't want to be standing there in his own stink when he gave her the bad news.

Bryce went back to the bathroom and stripped off his clothes, taking a few seconds to probe the tender, quarter-sized bruise on his left thigh. Until then, everything in the immediate aftermath of the hornet's sting had seemed like a dream, but seeing the evidence etched starkly into his skin made him realize just how close he'd actually come to dying. As he stepped into the tub, he closed his eyes and let the warm water flow over him. It felt good to be alive.

He'd just finished drying his hair when he

heard Melanie walk through the door. Bryce threw on his clothes and prepared himself to deliver the bad news. As he stepped out into the living room, he saw her standing in the kitchen, putting something in the oven. On the counter were a bouquet of mums, a loaf of bread, and a pie. Shep was dancing around her, hungry for attention. Watching the happy domestic scene, Bryce felt a tightness in the back of his throat. How could he ever have given all this up? he wondered. And what would it take to get it back?

"Hello, my baby," Melanie cooed, giving the dog a kiss. "Have you been taking good care of our patient?"

Bryce cleared his throat.

"You're home early."

She looked over at him and grinned.

"And you're up. How are you feeling?"

"Better."

He started toward her hesitantly. What was the protocol for greeting one's ex-spouse under the present circumstances? A kiss might be too much, but would a hug be acceptable? He'd just spent the night in her bed, too; even if she hadn't been in there with him, it still felt like a shared intimacy.

Melanie came over and took him by the arm.

"Come and see," she said. "Everyone in

town has been so nice. Francine made us a casserole and Walt brought over a loaf of Mae's rye bread. The flowers are from Ashley's garden.

"And," she said, holding the pie aloft, "Flora brought over one of her apple pies. She says you're forgiven for missing the bake sale."

Bryce looked at the bounty and marveled at everyone's generosity. Fossett might be down on its luck, he thought, but it was full of good people. Seeing how hard everyone had worked to help out, though, was only going to make delivering his bad news harder.

Melanie was hunting through the kitchen drawers.

"When did you get up?"

"About half an hour ago. I just got out of the shower."

She took out a paring knife and waved it like a baton. Bryce tried not to flinch as the blade slashed through the air.

"I thought I'd make us a salad. Once the casserole's heated, we can eat."

He reached out and took her arm.

"Hey," he said. "Can you hold on a second, and maybe . . . put the knife down? I need to talk to you."

She set the knife aside and looked at him.

"Sure. What's on your mind?"

Bryce paused to gather his thoughts. After their talk earlier, it felt as if they'd reached a new understanding. He hoped that what he said now wouldn't put that at risk.

"I have to leave. My office called a little while ago. There's an all-hands meeting tomorrow at nine."

Melanie gave him a curious look; for a moment, Bryce thought she might even laugh.

"You're not really thinking of going back there, are you? Not with Colton on the loose."

"Mel, I have to. It's my job."

Her face clouded over as she shook her head.

"No. You don't owe them your life."

Bryce set his hands gently on her shoulders.

"Please try and understand," he said. "You know I wouldn't go if I didn't have to, but I've already been AWOL for a couple of days. I can't afford to just blow it off."

"But how can they even think of calling you back? Don't they realize the danger you'll be in?"

She searched his face.

"You didn't tell them, did you?"

He shook his head.

"I should have, I know. I just —"

"Didn't tell them what they didn't want to hear."

Bryce nodded sheepishly.

"You're right. It's something I'm just not good at. I had my reasons, but I'm not sure you'd understand." He shrugged. "At this point, I'm not sure I understand them myself."

Melanie folded her arms.

"Is there anything else you're not telling me? About this?" She paused. "About us?"

He looked up sharply.

"No, I'm done with that. From now on, you'll hear the truth from me, even if I know you won't like it." He allowed himself a small smile. "Be careful what you wish for."

"It doesn't matter if I like it," she said. "As long as we're honest with one another."

She turned away, trying to get herself under control.

"I'm sorry I overreacted; I know you have to go. I'm just scared. It feels like I just got you back and now I'm losing you all over again."

He wrapped his arms around her waist and whispered in her ear.

"Yes, but you didn't lose me, and the police will find Colton soon. In the meantime, I promise I'll be careful. Try to have a little faith, will ya?"

Melanie nodded and broke free of his embrace. As she turned to face him, she was all business.

"You'll need to take my car."

"If you don't mind," he said. "Sorry."

Melanie rolled her eyes, even as tears started to well.

"Oh, *now* you're sorry."

The two of them shared a bittersweet laugh.

"It's not going to be the same as it was," Bryce said. "I promise. I don't want to live without you anymore."

She nodded and a single tear ran down her cheek.

"Just be safe," she said. "And come back to me. We can work out the rest."

Bryce gave her a kiss.

"I will," he said. "You can count on it."

Chapter 17

Traffic was miserable the next morning. By the time Bryce pulled into one of the underground parking spaces at Norcross Daniels, he was running late. He'd been tempted to use the SmartPark on Jefferson to avoid being seen in Melanie's car, but it would have meant a four-block hike to his building, and with Jesse Lee Colton still on the loose he didn't want to chance it. Better to take another ribbing from Asa than a bullet in the back. He stepped out of the old Honda and reached into the back seat for his coat.

"Oh no. Are you *kidding me?*"

The camel hair was covered in dog fur. Bryce slapped at it a few times, but the black and white hairs refused to budge. No matter, he thought. It wasn't as if he were going to wear it into the meeting. He'd stop by Gemma's desk later and see if she had one of those sticky roller things.

The sound of screeching tires alerted him to the approach of another car. Bryce saw a black Audi TT roar down the ramp and pull into a handicapped spot by the elevators. When the driver's door flew open, he saw Asa carefully hang a disabled parking permit on the rearview mirror before getting out. Bryce felt his nostrils flare.

What a jerk.

For a moment, he considered taking the stairs. The office might be on the tenth floor, but it'd be worth it not to be trapped in the elevator with Asa. He was still feeling the effects of the EpiPen, though, and even if he did make it all the way, he'd be sweaty and out of breath by the time he got to the meeting. He'd just have to grin and bear it.

Asa had already pushed the button when Bryce walked up. He glanced pointedly at the coat.

"Long time, no see," he said. "How was the vacay?"

"I was only gone for two days."

"I see you got yourself a new set of wheels, though." He looked back at the Honda and smirked. "You really outdid yourself this time, bro."

Bryce gritted his teeth. He'd been hoping the guy hadn't noticed.

"It belongs to a friend; mine's at the detailer."

Asa was watching the numbers over the door count down, looking oddly self-satisfied.

"A lot's changed around here since you left."

"Is that what this meeting's about?" Bryce said.

"It is indeed. The population of Norcross Daniels is about to increase by one."

The doors opened and the two of them stepped inside.

"Who is it, do you know?"

Asa moved his fingers across his mouth in a zippering motion.

"My lips are sealed."

Fine, Bryce thought; he'd find out soon enough. As the doors closed, he kept his mouth shut and stared straight ahead.

The meeting was being held in the large conference room. By the time they got there, the senior attorneys were already seated around the table and the paralegals were standing along the walls. Bryce grabbed a cup of coffee at the cart and took the last seat at the table. As he sat down, he felt a jolt of surprise. Sofia Cardoza was sitting directly across from him. He'd barely had time to consider the implications before

Preston Daniels walked in and called the meeting to order.

"I know we've all got work to do this morning," he said. "So I'll make this brief. After long and careful consideration, Norcross Daniels has hired its first senior female attorney: former municipal court judge Sofia Cardoza."

Sofia smiled and dipped her chin at the smattering of applause, most of which came from the paras.

"Sofia's exceptional work ethic is legendary and her history on the bench offers us a rare opportunity to gain insight into the jurist's point of view, but it's the impressive roster of new media clients she brings with her that we're especially excited about."

Daniels's admin passed through the room, handing each person a list of Sofia's clients. Bryce glanced at the first few names and set it aside. He'd look it over later.

"This is an amazing opportunity for all of us," Daniels continued. "Sofia's grasp of the unique challenges facing high-profile, media-savvy companies has positioned her to become one of the finest legal advocates in that sector on the West Coast, making her a magnet for the kind of new-economy clients Norcross Daniels will need as the legal landscape continues to evolve. With

Sofia Cardoza on our team, we'll be moving squarely into the twenty-first century and beyond."

Bryce took a sip of coffee to hide his smile. *This from a man who still referred to computers as "fancy typewriters."*

"Of course, every legal firm has its own unique way of doing things, and Sofia is anxious to get up to speed as soon as possible. Therefore — at her suggestion," he said, nodding in her direction, "I'm assigning one of you lucky young gentlemen to show her the ropes."

Bryce felt a kick under the table and saw Asa grin as he straightened his tie. So, that's what the guy had been so smug about, he thought. The old man must have given him a heads-up before the meeting. Ordinarily, showing a new hire the ropes would be left to an admin, but Sofia Cardoza was an important acquisition. After Daniels's effusive introduction, it was clear that whoever he assigned to squire her around would be seen as a man on the move. In spite of himself, Bryce felt a twinge of jealousy.

Well, better him than me, he told himself. Sofia might be beautiful, but she could be willful and impatient, too. Asa was going to have his hands full. Then Bryce glanced back at Daniels and felt a chill. The man was staring right at him.

"I know you two will want to get started right away, Bryce, so take the rest of the day to clear your schedule. Starting tomorrow, you'll be getting Sofia up to speed and putting together a support team so she can hit the ground running. Don't let us down."

Bryce was stunned. He'd promised Melanie he'd only be in town for one day; now he was committed to a week or more helping Sofia settle in. Not only that, but he had nowhere to stay. Going back to his condo was a nonstarter — if Colton could get into his building once, he could do it again — but driving back and forth from Fossett every day would be untenable. Nevertheless, it was an honor to be singled out by the boss, and when he saw the furious look on Asa's face he couldn't help feeling pleased.

As the room emptied, Bryce and Sofia remained seated, eyeing each other over their cups of coffee and sharing embarrassed smiles. Remembering Daniels's comment that she'd asked for someone to assist her, Bryce wondered if she'd also suggested that he be the one to do it. If so, things between them could easily turn awkward. He'd have to make it clear at the outset that their relationship would remain strictly platonic.

"So." Sofia grinned.

"So yourself." Bryce leaned forward. "Why didn't you tell me about this when I saw you last week?"

"I wanted to," she said. "But it would have been indiscreet to say anything in front of the others. If you had joined me for a drink like I asked, I would have."

Bryce felt his face warm, remembering how anxious he'd been to rebuff what he'd assumed was a come-on. Sofia was a beautiful woman whose personal style could be flirty — even seductive — at times, and wiser men than he had made the mistake of taking it seriously, to their detriment. He'd have to be careful not to read more into her behavior than was actually intended.

"I think Asa was counting on being the chosen one. When the old man picked me instead, he looked like he was ready to spit."

"Yes, I saw that." She giggled. "Poor thing."

"I have to confess, though, Daniels really threw me a curveball with this assignment. I've been out of town the last few days and it was a complete surprise."

"But where have you been?" She sobered. "Was it to do with Jesse Colton?"

Bryce hesitated. During the brief time that he and Sofia had been together she'd gotten an earful about the breakup with his ex-wife, and he wasn't sure how she'd react if he told her he was seeing Melanie again. He was still unsure about their future together, and at this point the two of them weren't even close to a full reconciliation. Better not to say anything than to try to justify something that might never be.

"An old friend asked me for some legal help," he said. "The chance to get out of town was serendipitous."

"But now you're back and Colton is still free." Her look was serious. "Surely, you're not planning to return home."

"No. Even with increased patrols in the area, I still don't feel safe going back to my condo."

Sofia reached for his hand.

"Then please, stay with me," she said. "Strictly as a friend. When I accepted the judgeship, my house was equipped with an alarm system tied directly to the police. I have a lovely guest bedroom; I'll even give you a key. You could come and go as you wish —"

"And if Colton found out where I was, we'd both be in danger." Bryce shook his head. "It's a generous offer, but I can't let you risk your life for mine. Colton's days as a free man are numbered. Until then, I'll just have to lie low and be patient."

She withdrew her hand.

"Of course. You must do what you think is best."

Sofia nodded, as if to say the matter was closed, but Bryce had a feeling it wouldn't be the last time they had this conversation.

"Is this your first official day at Norcross?"

She shook her head, releasing a cloud of perfume.

"Monday," she said. "Until then, however, there is much to do. I'll be counting on you to meet my needs."

Bryce nodded, reminding himself of his own good counsel. This was just Sofia being Sofia, unconsciously using a tactic he'd seen her employ in court to great effect when he was with the DA. When caught off guard, she used innuendo to distract and unnerve the competition while she considered her next move. In spite of Daniels's declaration that hers was a senior position, it had been a while since Sofia was a full-time advocate and Bryce would be willing to bet that much of her recent success had been in arbitration, rather than at trial. There was also the pressure of being a "first" at Norcross Daniels weighing on her. Not just the first senior woman, but the first Latina in a prestigious firm of conservative old white guys. Rather than worry about whether or not she was trying to beguile him, Bryce told himself, he should see her behavior as a form of self-defense.

"So," he said. "When do you and I get started?"

"Tomorrow. I am due in court at one o'clock this afternoon and there are still preparations to be made."

"Who's hearing your case?"

Sofia wrinkled her perfect nose.

"Samuel Hightower."

"Ouch. Looks like you drew the short straw."

Samuel Obadiah Hightower had been on the bench since dirt was young and he was about as close to being a "hanging judge" as there was in the state. A prosecutor's dream, he regularly gaveled down the objections of defense attorneys, and his repertoire of facial expressions was so obviously biased in favor of the prosecution that the bar association had twice sanctioned him for improper influence. Nevertheless, getting rid of the man had proved impossible. At this point, the city's defense lawyers were just running out the clock, hoping to avoid his courtroom until the man retired.

"Yours must be one of the last cases on his docket. I hear he's retiring at the end of the year."

"December the twenty-second," she said. "It had not escaped my notice."

Sofia tossed her head as if making her case in front of the hardest heart on the bench was nothing special.

"We have a good case," she said. "I am not afraid of that old man."

As she stood, Bryce had to admire her confidence, even if it was just whistling in the dark. He doubted even Sofia could charm Sam Hightower.

She smiled coquettishly.

"Until tomorrow, then."

He nodded.

"Until tomorrow."

Bryce felt a bit at sea as he returned to his office. Gemma had left a stack of messages on his desk and his in-box was overflowing. Even after only a few days away, the shock of being back in the pressure cooker was disorienting and he found himself reluctant to jump right back in.

He stood at the window and looked down at the city. Somewhere out there was a man who wanted to kill him just for doing his job. Sofia had assumed that he was afraid to go out in public, which was true. He was afraid of pain, afraid of being tortured the way Colton had tortured his other victims, afraid of dying before he'd had a chance to really live. But when he thought about Colton the man, it wasn't fear Bryce felt but contempt. Colton was from a good family, he was educated, he'd had advantages a lot of people didn't get, and yet he'd chosen to kill — and not only kill but also do it in a particularly heinous way. Having to exercise some caution until a man like that was back behind bars was a small price to pay for bringing him to justice.

Speaking of justice.

Bryce fished Melanie's keys out of his coat pocket. Maybe he'd just head over to Glen Wheatley's office and see what the latest was.

The increased police patrols around Mac-Donald's condo had done their job. Jesse Lee had tried several times to get back into the building, but the residents had been warned not to buzz anyone in without an ID and he'd had to abandon his efforts in favor of the second target on his list.

Spotting Vance Rowland at the dinner table had been a stroke of luck and shooting him in front of his wife and kids was especially satisfying, but after the first shot all hell had broken loose and Jesse had been forced to hightail it before the cops showed up. As he sat on the sidewalk outside Norcross Daniels that morning, he was still working on a plan to finish the job.

A man tossed a coin into the upturned hat and Jesse mumbled the obligatory, "God bless you." That was the funny thing about hiding in plain sight, he thought. Everyone had heard about it and no one believed it. Every man jack thought he could spot a fugitive if he saw one on the street, but even people who were good with faces drew a blank if you asked them to describe the homeless guy they passed every day on their way to work. Cops, of course, were better at it. When you saw the same folks day after day — how they moved, the places they hung out, their methods for wheedling a few bucks out of the public — it sort of stuck with you. That's why it had been important for Jesse Lee to look like one of the regulars; a new guy on the street would have been spotted in an instant.

But MacDonald was being extra cautious. Even with the stepped-up police patrols, he hadn't returned to his condo. Sooner or later, though, the man would have to go to his office, and as luck would have it, there was a homeless guy about Jesse Lee's height and weight whose regular spot was just a few steps from the building's parking garage — the perfect place to conduct surveillance. He'd simply followed the man back to his hovel one night and persuaded him to give up his clothing. And the hat, of course — the hat was important. By the time anyone found the man's body, Jesse would be long gone.

He heard a car coming up the ramp and ducked his head, turning his chin slightly so he could see the driver as it emerged without revealing too much of his own face. Chances were good that it wasn't his quarry; Mac-Donald rarely left work before six. Nevertheless, he felt a stab of disappointment when the old Honda came into view. Jesse turned away, reminding himself that surveillance was a long game. To win it, you had to be patient.

A woman in a pink coat walked up and stuck a dollar bill in his face.

"Here you go, young man."

Jesse didn't really care about the money, but if he was going to pull off his disguise he could hardly ignore her. As he raised his head to offer another compulsory blessing, the Honda turned in front of him and he got a good look at the driver.

MacDonald!

No wonder he hadn't seen the man's car that morning. He'd swapped his old BMW for an even older Civic. Was it a coincidence, he wondered, or had Bryce MacDonald done it deliberately to throw him off the scent? Either way, Jesse Lee had only seconds to memorize the car's details. As he snatched the bill from the woman's hand, he stared after the receding automobile, committing the Oregon license plate to memory along with the make, model, and color of the car. This was the break he'd been waiting for, he thought triumphantly. The first person on his hit list was almost within his grasp.

CHAPTER 18

Glen Wheatley didn't seem especially surprised to see Bryce. Sitting behind his desk, glasses perched low on his nose, he was reading something on his computer screen when Bryce knocked. Without looking up, he motioned toward the visitors' chair across from him.

"Be with you in a sec."

Bryce took a seat and looked around. The place looked exactly as it had the day he'd handed in his resignation over a year ago: same papers on the desk, same cardboard boxes stacked against the walls, same crappy, worn-out furnishings in a building that probably didn't even meet modern fire codes. The powers that be had promised they'd all be getting an upgrade once the new courthouse was finished, but that was years ago. At this point, he was sure that no one was holding their breath. A beam of sunlight broke through the clouds and landed just out of reach. Well, he thought, at least the place had a view.

At last, Wheatley turned away from the monitor and removed his glasses. The man looked as tired and harried as ever. Bryce wondered if he'd looked the same way when he worked there.

"Any word yet about Colton?"

The man shook his head and stretched his arms overhead.

"Depending on which of our informants you talk to, he's either living it up in Baja or passing himself off as a Latina down in Chinatown."

Bryce smirked. The thought of a racist homophobe like Jesse Lee dressed up as a Hispanic woman was almost funny.

"So," he said. "Which one do you be-lieve?"

"Neither. Colton wouldn't be caught dead in a dress and he's not going to leave until he's made good on his threat."

You mean until he tries to kill me.

"How's Vance?"

Wheatley held out a palm and waggled it.

"Still touch and go. There's another surgery scheduled for tomorrow. We'll know more after that."

Bryce nodded. He'd have to get down to the hospital while he was in town. Bev would have her hands full with the girls and he'd heard she was expecting again. He hoped her folks would be able to give her a hand.

"I hear Norcross Daniels has added Sofia Cardoza to its lineup. Congrats. She could have had her pick of firms."

"Yeah, the old man called an all-hands this morning just so he could crow about it."

Wheatley tried to hide a smile.

"And I hear he's made you her errand boy. That should be fun."

Bryce was annoyed at the characterization. Helping Sofia get acclimated might not be the most prestigious job, but that hardly made him her lackey, and the implication that his duties might include more intimate favors was insulting. He wondered if Asa was behind this.

"Where'd you hear that?"

The assistant DA shrugged noncommittally.

"Word travels fast."

"Well, believe me, working with her wasn't my idea. I came into town hoping for a quick turnaround and now I'm stuck here for god knows how long."

"Why not tell Daniels to give her to someone else? He must understand the predicament you're in."

"I'd rather not remind him about the whole Colton episode. He went out on a limb hiring a prosecutor; I can't afford to have him think that I'm attracting the wrong sort."

"Yeah, I forgot. You guys deal with a better class of criminal over there."

Bryce shook his head, refusing to be drawn into an argument. The two of them had been friends a long time.

"Anyway, because of this assignment, I'm going to be stuck in town for a couple of days. Any chance you could find me somewhere safe to hide out?"

Wheatley frowned.

"What about your place? We've still got extra patrols in the area."

"Come on, Glen. A patrol car making a couple of extra trips around the block is hardly going to stop someone as determined as Colton."

"Yeah," he said. "You're right."

"So, you'll find me something?"

Wheatley pushed a few papers around on his desk.

"All right, two days, tops. Any more than that and I'll be answering to the budget committee."

"Thanks, Glen. And look, if things change —"

Bryce heard a knock. The section's security guard was standing at the open door.

"We've had another one. Bomb squad wants everybody out while they check the building."

Wheatley's face reddened.

"Again?"

"Don't blame me," the woman said as she turned to leave. "I'm just passing along the message."

He shut down his computer and snatched his jacket from the back of a chair.

"Come on."

Bryce followed him down the hall.

" 'Again?' Has this been happening a lot?"

Wheatley opened the door to the stairwell and the two of them started down.

"Third time this year," he said. "Probably some joker wanting to delay his hearing."

Bryce checked his watch. The county courtrooms were downstairs on the first floor; Sofia was probably just arriving for her own hearing. Maybe she wouldn't be facing Judge Hightower after all.

Some people have all the luck.

They stepped out of the stairwell into a crowd of people pacing, smoking, talking on phones or to one another, while they watched the bomb squad prepare to search the building. As Bryce glanced around, he felt suddenly exposed. What if Colton had followed him there? Calling in a bomb threat would be an easy way to get him out into the open.

"Want to grab a coffee?"

Bryce shook his head.

"Nah, I'm fine. Probably best not to hang around out here too long."

Wheatley's laugh was brutal.

"If you're worried about Colton, don't be," he said. "When he comes for you, it'll be up close and personal."

Bryce left the courthouse and drove to the hospital to see how Vance was doing. After fighting his way through a crowd of agitated strangers, the monitored protection of a high-security facility was a relief. He signed in at the desk and submitted to two pat downs — one when he reached the ICU and a second, more invasive one outside Vance's room. As he waited for the guard to open the door, Bryce felt a flash of anger. With all the warning the police had been given after Colton's escape, it seemed impossible that he'd been able to reach his victim so easily. Where, Bryce wondered, had all this security been when his friend had been shot?

Vance looked pale and shrunken lying in the bed, hooked up to wires and surrounded by beeping monitors that kept a constant record of his vital signs. When Bryce stepped in, Bev was sitting in a chair next to the bed, one hand holding a book, the other resting on her husband's leg. As she stood to greet him, Bryce saw that she was indeed pregnant and wondered how she would bear it if Vance didn't pull through. He gave her a brief hug.

"How's he doing?"

"No change since yesterday," she said. "But the doctors are hopeful. They say they'll know more after the next surgery."

"How're you holding up?"

Bev shrugged.

"Not too bad, all things considered. They say the first couple of hours are the most important and we were lucky there was help nearby to get him here."

No doubt, they were both thinking the same thing: With help so close at hand, how had this happened in the first place? This, however, was neither the time nor place to be asking that question.

"How are the girls doing?"

"Better," she said. "My folks are staying at

the house, which is a big help, but I've taken them out of school for the time being and we're taking them to see a counselor. They were there, you know . . . at the table."

She glanced over at her husband, her chin trembling. Bryce felt his hands ball into fists, almost wishing Colton would show up so he could strangle him.

"They'll be okay," he said. "They're young, and the counselor will know what to do. Eventually, they'll be able to put it in perspective."

Bev nodded, blinking away her tears, and turned to face him.

"I know they will," she said. "I just don't know yet if I will."

There wasn't much more to say after that. Bryce told her he'd seen Glen Wheatley and urged Bev to call him if she needed anything, but Vance never opened his eyes and there wasn't any point in trying to wake him. Anything the guy might have been able to tell him about the attack had already been shared with the police.

He walked back out to the waiting room and asked the nurse if there was somewhere he could make a phone call. She pointed to a designated cell phone area near the stairwell. Bryce closed the door behind him and called Melanie. She sounded tired.

"Hey," he said. "How's it going?"

"Not bad. Just lots to do here trying to get the volunteers sorted out. When do you think you'll be back?"

Bryce grimaced.

"Not as soon as I'd thought, unfortunately. The firm hired a new senior member and I've been assigned to help" — he almost said *her* — "with the transition."

"Oh. I'm so sorry."

"No, I'm the one who's sorry. I've left you without a car *and* a campaign manager."

"But where are you going to stay? You're not going to go back to your condo."

"No, I talked to Glen Wheatley and he said they'd put me up in a secure location for the time being. With any luck, it'll only be for one night."

"Well, that's something, anyway."

Bryce paused as a voice over the intercom paged Doctor Chen.

"Sorry about the noise; I'm calling you from the hospital. I stopped by to see how Vance was doing. Bev was with him."

"How's she holding up?"

"Better than I'd expected — especially considering she's pregnant again."

"Oh, Bryce."

"Vance was out of it, though. Not sure if it's a coma or he's just sleeping, but he

230

looks pretty bad."

He ran a hand down his face, trying not to think about the man lying in bed just down the hallway. Even in the worst moments after the conviction, Bryce had never really believed that Colton would escape, much less that he'd actually try to carry out his threats.

"Listen, I'd better go. I'm hoping to be back tomorrow, but I'll call if anything changes. I'm really sorry to be leaving you in the lurch like this."

"Don't worry about it," she said. "We're all doing fine. You just stay safe and we'll see you when you get here."

Bryce hung up and slipped the phone back into his pocket, then walked back out to Melanie's car feeling like he had a target on his back.

Melanie felt a stab of guilt as she hung up the phone. In spite of what she'd told Bryce, things really hadn't been going very well that day. Only half the people who'd volunteered to canvass had actually shown up, and of those, two had said they couldn't work for more than an hour. Then Kayla had called, asking for the day off to finish a term paper, and after all the extra time she'd been putting in at the shop lately,

Melanie felt she couldn't say no.

Even some of the good things that had happened the day before had backfired on her. The people who'd come by to ask about Bryce had also eaten every muffin, scone, and Beavertail in her display case and Walt said that Mae wouldn't have any more for her until Friday. Melanie felt as if she'd been holding her breath until Bryce got back, and now he wouldn't be there for at least another day.

She went into the back room and took her lunch out of the refrigerator, feeling sorry for herself. Kayla was gone, Bryce wasn't coming back, and Shep was out canvassing with Flora Grieb. It felt like she'd been abandoned.

Look at you, sitting there feeling sorry for yourself. You're not helpless. There's still plenty of work to do before the election. Get to work.

Melanie set her mouth. Her better self was right: She wasn't helpless. There was a lot she could do. In fact, there was something she'd been wanting to do for a while but hadn't because she didn't want to step on Bryce's toes. Well, she thought, it was time to find out when his friend Dave Giusti was going to come out and do their interview. She got the number from Information and waited while his phone rang.

"Editorial. Giusti here."

"Hi. This is Melanie MacDonald. I'm a . . . friend of Bryce's."

"Friend," she thought, sounded better than "ex-wife."

"Uh-huh."

The guy sounded distracted. Melanie hoped she hadn't caught him at a bad time.

"I think Bryce contacted you about my dog, Shep, who's running for mayor out here in Fossett, and I was wondering —"

"I'm sorry, who did you say you were?"

"Oh, sorry," she said, feeling flustered. "My name is Melanie. Bryce MacDonald told me he called you to discuss setting up an interview with me and my dog and I was just wondering when we might be able to —"

"Uh, Melanie? I think there's been some sort of miscommunication here. I already told Bryce I'm not interested. No offense, but I don't do animal stories. If you want, I can give you the name of one of our stringers and you can see if he wants it, but like I told Bryce, this kind of story just isn't for me. Sorry to be so blunt, but that's just the way it is."

Melanie's face was burning.

"No, of course. I totally understand," she

said. "I'm sorry to have bothered you."

She hung up, feeling like a fool. Dave Giusti must have thought she was just hoping he'd change his mind if she badgered him enough. She was so embarrassed she felt like crawling into a hole. Why hadn't Bryce told her the truth instead of letting her think the interview was on?

Melanie swiped away an angry tear. Bryce had promised to tell her the truth from now on, no matter how upsetting, and yet when she'd asked if there were any other things he hadn't come clean about, he'd sworn there weren't. Maybe he'd simply forgotten, she thought. Or maybe he was counting on her not finding out. Maybe he'd even been trying to sabotage Shep's campaign all along, figuring that if her plan failed she'd give up on Fossett and return to Portland with him.

She was on the verge of calling him back and demanding to know what was going on when it occurred to Melanie that she'd done enough talking. She'd given Bryce a second chance and he'd blown it. Now it was time for her to do what she should have done all along: take charge. She reached into her pocket and took out the piece of paper Kayla had given her the day before.

This time, the man who answered the

phone didn't sound bothered when Melanie gave him her name. In fact, Chad Chapman seemed thrilled that she'd returned his call. After a brief chat while she told him about Shep and the situation in Fossett, he told her that he and his cameraman could be there in the morning to begin their interview.

"That would be perfect," Melanie told him. "I can't wait."

CHAPTER 19

Bryce had gotten a late start that morning. Not only had the "secure facility" Glen Wheatley promised him turned out to be a cheap room across the street from a rave club, but Sofia had insisted he drop by the office and help her with a problem that any admin could have easily taken care of. With only one day until Fossett's election, he knew that Melanie would be scrambling to get ready, and being held back by meaningless requests from a petulant senior attorney was infuriating. By the time he pulled out of the garage at Norcross Daniels, he was ready to leave and never come back.

He wondered how Melanie was doing. With luck, the volunteers had finished canvassing yesterday, which would leave only administrative details like getting voting booths set up and ballots checked and sorted left to do. In spite of his initial skepticism, Bryce had gotten caught up in the whole "Mayor Shep" idea, and though he had real misgivings about Melanie's plans beyond that, he did think that the gimmick itself could be useful.

Bryce had been thinking a lot the last two days about the time he'd spent in Fossett. The town had changed a lot in the last four years. Back then, it still had the rough-and-tumble feel of a timber town with little to offer beyond a dwindling number of good-paying jobs, and the thought of trying to raise a family there had been so appalling that Bryce simply couldn't believe that Melanie wanted to move back. But things were different now, and although it was true that the town was in a more precarious position, economically, than it had been, the things that could make it an attractive place to live were obvious. In many ways, in fact, it had become more like a place he'd want to settle down than where he was now. The challenge would be how to keep what was good about the town while reversing its economic decline.

If he were to move, there'd be challenges, of course. Fossett was too small to support a full-time attorney, but there were other small towns in the area that might make up the difference, and the DA's office in Corvallis might be happy to have him. The only question was, did Melanie really want him back?

As he drove, he'd been checking his rearview mirror periodically to make sure he wasn't being followed. The Honda had seemed like the perfect cover while he was in town, but there was always a chance that Colton had spotted him either going into work or leaving. But as the miles passed with no sign of anything suspicious around him, he started to feel the tension drop away, and by the time he passed Salem, Bryce figured he was home free.

He took the turnoff for Fossett, grinning like a kid on holiday. Not only would he be seeing Melanie again, but for a few precious hours he'd be free of the gnawing fear that had haunted him every second he'd been in Portland. As he pulled onto Main Street and headed for Ground Central, it felt almost like coming home. He couldn't wait to see Melanie and catch up on everything that had happened while he was away.

The first hint that something was wrong was the black Hummer parked in front of Melanie's shop. The tailgate was open and a large man in a T-shirt and jeans was taking out something that looked like a microphone stand. As Bryce pulled in at the curb, the man stepped away from the Hummer and dropped a coil of audio cable into a duffel bag on the ground. The logo on the front of the man's shirt said: INNOVATIVE MEDIA SOLUTIONS.

He felt a frisson of anxiety. Melanie hadn't mentioned anything about this last night.

The second sign that all was not well was the campaign poster in the front window. Bryce pressed his lips together. He thought that Melanie had understood the need to keep Shep's campaign and her workplace separate. Was this just something an overeager volunteer had put up by accident, or had it been done deliberately? And if so, what had happened to change her mind? Then he got out of the car and saw a CLOSED sign on the front door. Whatever this was, Bryce thought, it definitely wasn't good.

The front door wasn't locked. Bryce walked inside and saw Melanie standing at the counter talking to a slim blond man who looked as if he'd just stepped off the pages of *GQ*. In spite of the wintry weather, he was wearing a polo shirt, its collar upturned, summer-weight slacks, and a turquoise sweater that was draped over his shoulders in a way that set off his summer-worthy tan. Considering that it was barely above freezing outside, Bryce thought the outfit looked ridiculous. As Bryce came closer, the two of them stopped talking and turned toward him. The man regarded him with amused curiosity.

"Why don't you finish your tea, Chad?" she said. "I'll be back in a second."

Melanie motioned for Bryce to follow her across the room.

"What's going on?" he hissed. "Who is that guy?"

She turned and gave him a pert look.

"That 'guy' happens to be Chad Chapman. He's the reporter who did the piece about the cat in England."

Bryce glanced at the fop sipping tea at the counter. He had the sort of too-perfect features that translated well to the small screen but seemed almost freakish in real life.

"What's he doing here?"

"He called and said he'd like to do a story about the election." She gave him a tight smile. "I thought it was a good idea."

Bryce ran a hand through his hair, feeling bewildered. When he'd spoken to her last night, it seemed as if Melanie couldn't wait for him to return. Now it was like she didn't even want him there. Why the sudden change?

"I thought we agreed not to accept any

unsolicited offers from unknown sources."

"He's not 'unknown,' " she said, making air quotes to emphasize the point. "I told you, I saw him on the television."

The look he gave her was deeply skeptical. Melanie was not usually so gullible.

"So, he just called you out of the blue with an offer of free publicity, is that it?"

Melanie's smile faltered.

"Well, yes."

"And that didn't strike you as odd? I mean, Fossett is pretty small potatoes. I find it hard to believe that a legitimate reporter would want to come all the way out here unless he had some ulterior motive."

"Why?" she said. "Because your friend *Dave* wouldn't do it?"

The comment landed like a punch to the gut. Bryce grimaced.

"I'm sorry. I was going to tell you when I got here, but when I saw all of this" — he made a gesture encompassing Chad, the man in the Hummer, and the pile of equipment on the floor — "it slipped my mind."

Melanie gave him a contemptuous look.

"Oh, so you were going to tell me, just not now?" She laughed. "Boy, does that sound familiar."

"Look, I said I was going to tell you. I just got thrown off by all this . . . stuff."

241

"Well, pardon me if I don't believe you. You see, I thought we had an agreement, and then last night when I called Dave, I found out that you'd already broken it."

Her face flushed as her lower lip began to tremble.

"I can't even tell you how embarrassed I was. The guy acted like I was some publicity-seeking weirdo."

Bryce shook his head. Dave always sounded like that on the phone. The guy had probably been in the middle of something when she called.

"I seriously doubt that's what he thought, but if he did, it was my fault. I'd only just called him the day before."

"Then why didn't you tell me instead of letting me make a fool of myself?"

She glanced at Chad, who looked as if he was absorbing every word.

"I don't want to talk about this here."

Bryce felt his temper flare. He was already operating on very little sleep and the whole reason he'd had to rush down there that morning was so he could help her out. Having Melanie try to turn this around and make it his fault was galling. He turned and gave Chad a friendly little wave.

"Any chance you could give us a minute here?"

"Bryce," Melanie hissed. "Stop it."

"No," Chad said breezily. "It's fine."

He grabbed a parka that was hanging by the door.

"Think nothing of it. I'll be in the Hummer whenever you're ready."

Bryce waited for the door to close before turning back toward Melanie.

"First of all," he said. "I already told you that I'd take care of it, so technically it wasn't your job to be calling Dave. I also think you're blowing this way out of proportion. Yes, it might have been better if I'd told you when we talked last night, but I'd just stepped out of a hospital room where a friend's life is hanging by a thread and it was a little hard to think when it could just as easily have been me lying there. So, I'm sorry if you were embarrassed, but that really isn't my fault."

Melanie folded her arms and stared him down.

"That still doesn't change the fact that you lied to me — again."

Bryce threw his hands in the air and turned away. What the hell was wrong with her? Had she not heard a single thing he said? He'd spent the better part of the last two days itching to get back to Fossett, ready to start on the life it seemed the two of them were ready to build together, and instead he'd found himself overruled and unjustly accused of violating an agreement he found ridiculous on its face.

"Fine," he said, turning back. "You want honesty? Here's some honesty for you. This whole plan you've got for 'saving' Fossett by returning it to its glory days is a big, fat mistake."

Melanie drew back, her mouth open. She couldn't have looked more startled if he'd slapped her face.

But Bryce hadn't finished.

"You can make Shep the mayor, if you want, but it's never going to fix what's wrong around here."

As the initial shock wore off, she clenched her jaw, glaring at him defiantly.

"And what makes you an expert all of a sudden? Don't forget, this is my hometown. I came back because someone needed to save it and I was the only one willing to do it."

"Are you sure? Because I look around here and I don't see a lot of people looking to be saved, Mel. I see people who are doing pretty well."

Her laugh was explosive.

"Doing well? Oh, my god, did you not see those kids playing in the streets? You think they're doing *well*?"

"Playing in the streets isn't the same as living in them. They have homes and parents who love them."

"They live in *hovels.*"

"Which is more than they'll be living in if you insist on filling this place with people whose only interest is cheap labor and cheaper land. You know what the Leaky Faucet Saloon was when timber was booming? A place where men spent their paychecks on liquor and gambling before they went home and beat their wives."

She waved her hands as if fending him off.

"You're exaggerating."

"A little, maybe, but not much, and people certainly didn't take their kids in there for dinner like they do now. This grand scheme you have to turn back the clock might just snuff out the tiny spark that's trying to catch fire here. I really think you need to consider what you're doing before you continue down this path."

"Of course I've considered it," she said. "I've been considering it for four years. You act as if I just woke up yesterday and thought, 'Gee, maybe I should do something.'"

"That's not what I mean. I know you've

been working on this. I can see the changes you've made, but they haven't made a difference, have they?"

She shook her head.

"No."

"Well, have you ever asked yourself why?"

Her eyes glistened.

"Because it's hard to change. Because the people who were left behind need someone to lead them."

Bryce pointed at her.

"You see there? That's the difference between you and me, Mel. You look around and see people who want someone to tell them what to do. I see people with talent and skill who just need someone to show them how they can make a living doing it. This is a new economy, Melanie. You've got everything you need to help Fossett become an incubator for what could be several small businesses. Don't destroy it by trying to return to the good old days."

"How dare you accuse me of that? Everything I've done is for them."

"Is it? Or have you been doing it for yourself?"

Melanie's face was red.

"*Myself?* You think giving up everything and moving back here was *easy*? You think working long hours without a break, without any help or even a vacation, is *selfish?*"

"I think you like being a martyr. I think you like having people do what you want and it really doesn't matter to you if they do it because it's what they want or because they feel sorry for you or because it's just easier to go along with you than to swim against the tide."

"Oh, please."

"You ever wonder why you don't like Rod Blakely?"

"Why should I? The guy's an ass."

She turned to walk away and Bryce stepped in front of her.

"No, you don't get to leave it at that. I'm serious, Mel. Have you ever given a serious thought as to what it is, exactly, that you don't like about the man?"

"You said it yourself: He argues with everyone. All the time about everything. I'm not the only one in town who doesn't care for him, either, so don't try and single me out like I'm making things up."

"Okay. Fair enough. And yet who was it who insisted that you hold an election instead of just making Shep the mayor?"

"He did; I told you that."

"Why?"

"Because he said it wasn't fair not to." Melanie huffed in exasperation. "I told you all this before."

Bryce leaned forward, willing her to see the point he was trying to make.

"Yes, but why did you agree to do it? You've already said you didn't want to, that doing something quickly was important. I even told you it'd be easier to just to make Shep the honorary mayor and forget about holding an election."

"So?"

"So, the question is: Why did you agree to put it to a vote?"

"I told you. Because Rod said it wasn't fair."

"No! It was because everyone else agreed with him, Mel. Can't you see? Rod Blakely stood up to you and there was nothing you could do because for once you couldn't railroad everyone into doing what you wanted. And *that's* why he gets under your skin. Because while everyone else just goes along, smiling and agreeing to whatever little scheme you come up with, Rod Blakely is the only one who dares to challenge you. That's why you don't like him."

Melanie stood there sullenly, looking like a teenager who'd just been grounded.

"Are you finished?"

Bryce deflated. It felt as if everything he'd been holding inside since the divorce had suddenly come bubbling up, leaving him hollowed out inside. For a moment, he'd thought it would help, thought she might even try to understand what he was telling her, even if she didn't agree, but he could see now that it had all been for nothing. He'd taken his best shot and missed.

"Yeah. I am."

He reached into his pocket and handed her the keys to the Honda.

"Thanks for the loaner. I can walk to Pete's from here."

CHAPTER 20

For several minutes, Melanie was too stunned to cry. How could Bryce have said those things to her? What did he know about the sacrifices she'd made? Where had he been when she was spending long days at the shop and long nights with Walt and the other town leaders brainstorming ways to pull Fossett back from the brink? Bryce had spent only four days there and suddenly he thought he knew the answer that had eluded her for four *years*? How dare he?

And yet she couldn't deny that he'd posed some uncomfortable questions. Why hadn't the things they'd done to revive the town been working? She'd been sure that every improvement the town made had been mutually agreed upon, too, but when she thought about it, Melanie realized there hadn't been a single one that wasn't her suggestion. Was it really possible that she was the only person in town with good ideas, or had everyone else been too cowed by her force of will to propose something of their own? The thought that she might have been browbeating her friends and neighbors all these years was sobering.

And there was something else, too. Something she'd been trying to hide from herself all morning. Shep wasn't enjoying working on this video. He'd been his usual hammy self the day before, fetching toys and doing tricks, but when Chad insisted he stay inside and not dirty his coat, the border collie had started to rebel. They were just small things, at first. He'd picked up the wrong toy a couple of times that morning, and once when Chad wanted him to paw the air on cue he'd rolled over instead, but Melanie told herself that Shep had probably just misunderstood the command. For the last hour, though, the mistakes had been more serious and she'd begun to suspect they were actually being done deliberately.

But what could she do now? Chad and Mick were almost through. Surely, her dog could hold out a few more hours, and then he could run and play outside as much as he wanted to.

She heard the click of nails on the concrete floor as Shep came padding around the counter, a toy dangling from his mouth. As he walked up and dropped it into her lap, Melanie's face crumpled.

Mr. Stuffy.

She threw her arms around the dog's neck and burst into tears.

"Oh, Shep, what if Bryce was right? What if all of this is just going to make things worse? I said such mean things to him. He'll never forgive me."

She heard the bell on the front door ring and quickly dried her face. Whether or not she'd made the right decision giving Chad the okay to come to Fossett, the work was almost finished. Chad had told her that morning that it would be their last day of shooting. *What's done is done,* she thought. The fight with Bryce had nothing to do with what Chad and Mick were doing. The two of them had been working hard to produce a video showcasing Shep's run for mayor and she should be grateful. At the very least, it would be fun to see her dog on the television. There was no choice now but to finish what she'd started.

There was a knock on the counter.

"Everything okay in here?" Chad said.

Melanie took a calming breath and tried to sound cheerful.

"I'm fine. I'll be out in a minute."

"Is Shep back there with you?"

She looked at the collie and gave him another hug.

"Yeah. We were just having a mutual support session."

"Well, Mick is almost done out here, so your boy needs to be camera-ready ASAP. Coat brushed, collar on, eyes clear — you know the drill. Chop-chop."

"Got it."

As she said it, Melanie realized that Shep wasn't the only who was getting tired of Chad's high-handedness.

"We'll be ready when you are."

She went to the sink and splashed cold water on her face. Calling Chad may not have been prudent, but she still believed that the story he was doing would improve Fossett's prospects and she was determined to see it through. Even if every other idea she'd had hadn't worked, that didn't mean that this one wouldn't. She wasn't going to quit this close to the finish line.

Melanie handed Mr. Stuffy back to Shep and the two of them walked out to the table where she kept his brush and "wardrobe" of collars and props. Soon, TV audiences all over the country would be falling in love with her dog. And after the vote tomorrow, she thought, as she snapped the shirt collar around his neck and straightened his tie, he'd be a terrific mayor, too.

While Shep was getting ready, Mick had been setting up the final shot — the one showing Mayor Shep conducting business at his desk. In the middle of the scene was a wooden desk, on which a small American flag and a brass nameplate that said: MAYOR had been placed. On the wall behind it was a green screen — a six-by-seven-foot sheet of bright green cotton that hung from a thin metal rod suspended between two spindly-looking stands. This, she'd been told, would allow Chad to fill in the rest of Shep's "office" during post-production.

Surrounding the simple scene, however, was a forest of equipment that took up more than half of the coffee shop's dining area. Light diffusers that looked like white umbrellas atop spindly black stands; a soft diffuser that resembled a veiled black shroud; a video camera mounted on a tripod; a boom mic, a shotgun mic, and a third mic that could be used to cancel any stray sounds from the street; and snaking through it all was a mass of cables and wires that made a trip to and from Shep's position behind the desk akin to walking through a minefield. Nevertheless, Melanie thought, they'd gone over his "script" several times at home and each time her collie's performance had been flawless. All Shep had to do was hang in there for a few more takes and it would all be over.

Mick gave a nod and Chad pointed to the small black leather office chair sitting behind the desk.

"We'll need the dog to take his mark."

Melanie looked down and gave Shep a nod.

"Okay, you know what to do. Let's go."

As they started forward, ready to make their way through the maze of cables, light stands, and mics, Chad stepped forward and snatched Mr. Stuffy out of Shep's mouth.

"We don't need this in the scene," he said.

Shep whimpered as the doll was tossed aside.

"Sorry," Melanie said. "That was my fault. I was going to take it when we got to the desk."

She looked down and stroked the collie's head.

"Don't worry. You can have Mr. Stuffy back in a minute."

Chad sauntered back to his place behind the camera and crossed his arms.

"Come on, boy," Melanie said.

She patted the leather chair, keeping it steady with the other hand.

"You know how to do this."

Shep leaped up and sat down in the chair while Mick adjusted the camera lens.

"How does it look?" Chad said.

The cameraman shook his head.

"We've got light coming in from the window. I'll have to grab a reflector from the van."

Chad sighed.

"How long will that take?"

"Five, ten minutes. Not long."

"Fine." He looked up at Melanie. "Let's take a short break."

"Okay."

She got Shep down from the chair and the two of them walked back to the table to wait. Shep grabbed Mr. Stuffy and went off to sulk in his bed.

Mick was at the door.

"Someone here to see you."

Melanie turned and saw Walt standing at the window.

"Hi, Walt! Hold on a second."

She made her way across the room, careful not to disturb the web of interconnected equipment, and stepped outside.

Walt peered over her shoulder, raising an eyebrow at the nameplate on the desk.

"Isn't that a bit presumptuous?"

"I know," she said. "But they have to finish shooting today. If Rod wins, I'm sure they'll cut out that part."

She smiled sheepishly. The excuse sounded lame even to her ears.

He glanced in Chad's direction.

"Have you got a second?"

"Oh, sure."

When Walt made no move to come inside, Melanie grabbed her coat and joined him on the sidewalk.

"What's on your mind?"

He looked away, shaking his head for a moment, then faced her squarely.

"I'm concerned about this business," he said, nodding in Chad's direction. "What's this movie, or whatever it is, supposed to be about?"

"Well," she said. "It's about Shep and how he's running for mayor and what that'll mean for Fossett. As far as I can tell, it'll sort of a promotional video about the town."

He gave her a skeptical look.

"Are you sure? I mean, has this guy said that in so many words?"

Melanie thought about that for a second. Had Chad actually told her what the focus of the story was?

"Not specifically, but we've talked about it a couple of times and I feel pretty confident that he's on the right track." She frowned. "Why?"

"Well, for starters, people have been coming into the store telling me that he's been asking a lot of personal questions — things that don't have anything to do with the town. And they've been filming in places that don't put Fossett in a very good light, like Little Russia and Lou Tsimiak's junkyard."

"Oh," she said. "Well, those are part of the town. I suppose it's only fair —"

But Walt wasn't going to be put off.

"They've been strutting around here like they own the place, too, taking advantage of folks' good nature. The big guy walked into Fossett House yesterday, ate up all of Selma's Beavertails and two pieces of Flora's apple pie, and walked out without paying. We're generous people around here, but these two are taking advantage."

Melanie was embarrassed. She'd been providing them both with free drinks and snacks since they got there. Mick had probably just assumed that everything in town was on the house. Still, the guy should have at least made the offer to pay.

"I'm so sorry, Walt. Believe me, I had no idea that any of that had been going on. I'll say something to both of them right away. Please tell everyone how sorry I am."

His expression softened.

"I know it's not your fault. I just thought you ought to know. The sooner these two hit the road, though, the happier I'll be. At this point, I just want to hold the election and put this whole episode behind us."

Melanie felt a pang. This whole episode, as he'd called it, was a direct result of her suggestion that Shep be the town's mayor. Once again, she thought, the folks in town were paying the price for one of her big ideas.

"Don't worry," she said. "I'll talk to Chad and make sure he understands what we're expecting from the video. In the meantime, maybe you could let everyone know that I'm sorry if they've been inconvenienced."

"I'm sure they'll understand," he said. "I know we all want good things to come from this."

Walt had been about to leave when he pulled up short.

"Oops! I almost forgot," he said. "Mae sent this along for Shep."

He reached into his pocket and took out a homemade dog treat.

"Here you go," he said, handing it to her. "Peanut butter and oatmeal."

Melanie shook her head.

"No, why don't you give it to him? We're on a break and he's been having a tough day. I'm sure he'd like to see you."

"Are you sure it's okay?"

She glanced through the front window. Mick was still adjusting the reflector.

"They're still getting ready in there. I'm sure it'll be fine."

As the two of them stepped inside, she saw that Shep was still lying in his dog bed, his head resting on Mr. Stuffy.

"Hey, Shep. Look who's here."

Walt held out the treat.

"Special delivery for the movie star," he said, holding out the treat. "Peanut butter and oatmeal — your favorite."

The collie got up and sidled over, his mouth already forming a doggie-style grin.

"Ah-ah-ah!"

Chad snatched the homemade treat from Walt's hand and set it on the counter.

"Treats are for dogs who finish their work," he said. "He can have this when we're done."

"You're right," Melanie said. "I wasn't thinking."

Walt turned and gave Melanie a hurt look.

"I'm sorry," she whispered. "It's just for now."

Mick had taken his place behind the camera.

"All right," Chad announced. "Time for

Shep to take his mark."

Melanie gave Walt another sheepish look and stepped forward.

"Okay," she said, checking to make sure Shep's tie was straight. "Come on, boy. Let's get you into place."

For just a moment, it looked as if the dog would comply. Compared to the things he'd been asked to do lately, it was easy: sit behind the desk and do a few simple tricks while Melanie prompted him from behind the camera. Instead, he balked. Perhaps he was bored with doing the same tricks over and over or maybe he was tired of being forced to stay indoors, but for whatever reason, Shep had had enough. He glanced from the unreachable treat to the man who'd taken it away and charged directly into one of the umbrella-topped stands.

"What's he doing?" Chad screeched.

As the light stand fell, it hit the next one in line, and the two came crashing down, their bulbs bursting with a sound like party poppers.

Melanie was horrified.

"Shep, stop!"

But the collie wouldn't listen; he was running amok. Shep grabbed a cable in his mouth and shook it violently. The stand holding the boom mic began to teeter.

"My equipment!"

Mick grabbed the camera as the boom mic came crashing down.

Chad was livid.

"Grab him! Get him out of there!"

Melanie made a lunge for Shep, but shattered glass and a jumble of fallen equipment were slowing her down.

"I'm trying!"

As the third light diffuser toppled over, she heard laughter and saw Walt holding his sides, howling as tears ran down his face.

But Shep wasn't through. As he leaped from the office chair onto the desk, the force of his takeoff sent the chair flying into the green screen, bringing the entire rig crashing to the ground.

"Walt!" Melanie begged. "Don't just stand there. Do something!"

"You want me to do something?" he said. "Okay, I'll do something."

He walked over to the counter, picked up the treat, and gave an ear-piercing whistle. The border collie turned and dropped the cable from his mouth.

"Here, Shep," Walt said, tossing the treat high into the air. "Catch!"

And Shep did.

CHAPTER 21

Bryce had finally cooled off by the time he got back to Portland. As the miles passed, his mood had changed from self-righteous indignation to chagrin. He shouldn't have lost his temper, he thought. If he'd only admitted his mistake in not calling Dave Giusti sooner, the whole thing could have been avoided. Melanie wouldn't have gotten embarrassed and there'd have been no need to call Chad Chapman. The only problem was, not calling Dave sooner hadn't been a mistake.

Melanie was right when she accused Bryce of trying to sabotage her plans. Not at first, of course. When he'd taken off for Fossett, his motivation had been purely selfish — to be free from the threat posed by Jesse Lee Colton. But once he'd seen Melanie, and especially after dinner that first night, Bryce had started to think there was a chance he might convince her to move back to Portland and patch things up. Helping spread the news about Shep's mayoral run could have delayed or even destroyed his chances.

But then Rod Blakely had gotten the jump on them, canvassing homes and spreading rumors about Shep that worried Melanie so much she was considering taking drastic action to garner publicity for Shep's cause. Offering to call Dave had been an act of desperation, something to keep Melanie from trying something on her own. Bryce's excuse, that she could be taken in by a scam artist, was true as far as it went, but his main concern had been to slow things down enough that he'd have time to convince her to give him another chance. By the time he'd changed his mind and actually called Dave, he was back in Portland, caught up in the changes brought on by Sofia's arrival. It was just rotten luck that Melanie had called Dave herself before Bryce could give her the bad news. Nevertheless, it didn't change one fundamental fact.

Melanie's right. I'm no good at giving bad news.

Even so, Bryce thought, as he checked through his in-box, there was a big difference between avoiding an uncomfortable truth and telling a lie. Communications between loved ones weren't legal proceedings, and in his opinion there was nothing to be gained from complete honesty with a spouse or lover, especially when feelings could be hurt — Exhibit A being the disaster his "honest" assessment of her Fossett improvement plan had been. Whether or not he was right, there had certainly been kinder ways to tell her than the way he'd done it. For a man who could keep his cool in the middle of high-stakes courtroom proceedings, he'd sure done a lousy job of presenting his case.

However, none of that negated what now appeared to be undeniable: As much as he loved Melanie — as much as they might love each other — there was too great a gap between them. She would never stop trying to save her hometown and he would never be able to make a life for himself down there. It simply was what it was.

The rest of the afternoon was taken up with getting his clients transitioned to other team members and replaying the disastrous confrontation with Melanie, and as the adrenaline-fueled self-talk diminished and the effects of too little sleep caught up with him, exhaustion set in. Bryce's eyelids became heavier and his yawns more frequent. He was on the verge of putting his head on the desk when Sofia knocked on his door.

"Wake up, sleeping head."

Bryce blinked groggily, smiling at her clumsy vernacular — something he suspected she cultivated.

"How'd the arbitration go?"

Sofia made a gesture that conveyed both frustration and disgust.

"No decision yet. Continuation until next week."

He nodded. Continuations were always a headache during arbitration. It meant the judge was considering setting it aside.

"What's the problem?"

She sighed dramatically.

"Please, could we discuss this over dinner? Unless you have other plans."

As Bryce considered the question, he suddenly realized that the gnawing in his stomach was more than emotion's denouement. Even so, he hesitated. With Colton still at large, would being out in public be too much of a risk?

"No. No other plans, but . . ."

"Don't worry," she said. "You'll be safe."

Sofia opened her purse and showed him the Walther P38 semi-automatic pistol inside.

"I'm a very good shot."

■ ■ ■ ■

They had dinner at a little place on the east side that served what Sofia swore was the most authentic Catalan cuisine in the city. From the outside, it looked like any one of the dozens of bistros that had sprung up in the area, but stepping inside was like entering another world — one that seemed both familiar and exotic. When Bryce commented on it, Sofia looked pleased.

"It is like the women of my country. No matter how well you know us, there remains always a little mystery."

As they waited for a table, Sofia pointed out the symbols of Catalonia displayed on the walls, touching him repeatedly on the arm, the shoulder, and the chest. Bryce knew by now not to take it seriously. Nevertheless, after all the effort he'd expended trying to win Melanie back, it felt good to be petted and fussed over by a beautiful and attentive woman. As the men at the bar sized him up, he felt a flush of unearned pride.

The hostess appeared and showed them to a booth in back over which a picture of the Madonna and child presided. Sofia crossed herself and genuflected quickly before taking her seat. As she shook out her napkin, she nodded toward the image.

"Our patroness," she said. "The Virgin of Montserrat."

A waiter approached with their menus and she swatted them away.

"I will order for us," she told him. "This is my treat."

Bryce leaned across the table.

"There's no need," he said. "This is business; the firm will pay."

"The firm can pay if it wishes, but I will not allow you to order *hamburguesa*." She sneered. "Tonight, you eat like a Catalan."

He sat back and laughed.

"Very well. I'm at your mercy."

The feast began with tapas: slices of rustic bread rubbed with fresh tomato and drizzled with olive oil and sea salt, a spicy sausage called *butifarra,* and Kalamata olives, marinated in oil and roasted red peppers. To drink, Sofia ordered Inedit Damm, a dark beer with hints of licorice, coriander, and orange peel.

"What do you think?" she said as Bryce took a sip. "Is wonderful, yes?"

He licked his lips, savoring the aftertaste.

"Very good. It reminds me of —"

"Nothing. There is nothing like it in the whole world."

Bryce nodded. It was no use arguing with a partisan.

"You're right. This beer is sui generis."

She reached over and squeezed his cheeks playfully.

"Look at you. Such a good little lawyer, with your Latin. Here," she said, signaling for the waiter. "Let me get you another."

Bryce rubbed a hand across his face, feeling faintly annoyed. He was too old to be having his cheeks pinched, and he wasn't comfortable with this overt possessiveness. Helping Sofia settle in at Norcross Daniels didn't mean she could treat him like her boy toy. He'd thought she wanted to talk about business.

"So," he said. "This continuation . . ."

He popped another olive in his mouth.

"What's the problem?"

She shook her head.

"The other party is trying to break an agreement they find troublesome. The judge is simply being difficult."

Bryce hid a smile. How many times, he wondered, had Sofia herself been described as difficult when she was on the bench?

He took another sip of the beer. The taste was beginning to grow on him.

"Is this one of your famous new media clients?"

She nodded.

"Innovative Media Solutions," she said. "More specifically, one of their employees."

Sofia topped another piece of bread with *butifarra*.

"Daniels was *so* impressed with my client list. If only he knew what some of these people are like."

She took a bite and swooned.

"Ah, this is heaven."

The name caught Bryce's attention. Hadn't he just seen it somewhere? Yes, it was on the T-shirt Chad's cameraman was wearing.

"It isn't Chad Chapman, is it?"

She raised an eyebrow.

"You know him?"

"No, but I have a friend who's working with him."

Sofia shrugged.

"Then they have my sympathy," she said. "The man has built a reputation on the destruction of others'."

As Bryce was considering whether or not to share this information with Melanie, the waiter appeared with a tray of *croquetas,* the Catalan version of croquettes.

"Doesn't that bother you?" he said.

But Sofia was more concerned at that moment with pointing out the delicacies in front of them.

"These two are eggplant and goat's cheese," she said. "The oval ones are mushrooms, pumpkin, and potato."

She paused, her eyes glittering as she decided which one to try first.

"Why should it bother me?"

Bryce was perplexed. It seemed like an obvious question, to him. Why would anyone want to work with, much less defend, someone they considered repugnant?

Sofia reached for a *croqueta,* so small and dark it looked burnt.

"And these," she said, "are squid, prawns, and squid ink."

He felt his stomach lurch.

"Ink?"

"Don't be a child," she said. "Try it."

Bryce bristled. He was beginning to regret his decision to accept her invitation. Not only was Sofia's attitude peremptory, but her unquestioning defense of someone like Chad Chapman struck him as almost immoral.

The waiter set two stemmed glasses in front of them and poured a bit of wine for her approval.

"Yes. Very good," she said, turning back toward Bryce. "Marqués de Cáceres is my favorite rosé. It goes very well with *croquetas.*"

Reluctantly, Bryce reached for his glass and took a sip. Was this the way the entire evening was going to go, he wondered, with Sofia giving the orders and him following along like a well-trained dog? He smiled, remembering the way Melanie's border collie had torn off Mr. Stuffy's head.

Shep wouldn't have put up with this crap.

"I see you smiling," Sofia purred. "You like it, yes?"

He took another sip of wine and let it roll around on his tongue while he considered his response. The wine was good, but not exceptional, an opinion he was loath to give under the circumstances. He decided to just tell the truth and hope it derailed this wearisome demand for encomium. Bryce swallowed and set down his glass.

"I was thinking about my friend's border collie, Shep. I had no idea they were so smart."

Sofia shrugged a shoulder.

"Really? I find dogs rather stupid, myself."

Bryce was surprised by how much her response rankled. Who did she think she was?

If Sofia suspected how her comment had affected him, though, it didn't show. She was too busy stage-managing his next move.

"Let us have no more talk," she said. "Try the *croquetas* — and finish your wine. There is still the Opera Prima to accompany our dinner and Don Luciano cava with dessert — very citrusy and light."

Bryce gaped at the bottle on the table. When Sofia had ordered their dinner, he assumed the wine would be served by the glass. Now he realized that she'd requested three entire bottles of wine in addition to the *cerveza* they'd had with their tapas. He chuckled nervously.

"If I didn't know better, I'd say you were trying to get me drunk."

"Oh no," she said. "You mustn't accuse me of such a thing. I only wanted you to experience what Catalunya has to offer. I feel we have been misunderstood."

As he turned his attention to the tray of *croquetas,* Bryce felt a prick of anxiety. First there'd been the touching and teasing, then the abundance of alcohol, and now this ambiguous declaration. The evening was starting to feel less and less like a business dinner and more like a date. Was it Sofia's country that was misunderstood, he wondered, or herself?

Sofia was watching him over her glass.

"How are your new accommodations?"

Bryce shook his head. He already knew where this was going.

"Not too bad. I may talk to Glen and see if they can move me someplace quieter, though."

Her look was sly.

"My offer still stands, you know."

He nodded, feeling almost relieved. At least the purpose of this evening was out in the open now. Perhaps he'd suspected all along that shop talk wasn't on the agenda, Bryce thought. Maybe he'd just been looking for some way to soothe his bruised ego.

Now, though, it was time to turn their conversation around, and Sofia had given him the perfect opening.

"Speaking of Glen Wheatley, I dropped by his office yesterday afternoon," he said. "Did that bomb threat affect your arraignment?"

Sofia hesitated, apparently unwilling to be thrown off track. She began picking through the *croquetas.*

"Oh yes. We had to reschedule for January."

"So, no Judge Hightower, huh? Wow. What were the chances?"

She gave him a steely look.

"You don't get to where I am by relying upon chance."

Bryce felt a chill. Sofia hadn't called in the threat herself, had she? Surely not. And yet . . .

And yet there'd been rumors before about Sofia's questionable ethics. Nothing that would warrant disbarment, but red flags nonetheless. Threatening to bomb a federal building — even in jest — was a felony.

"Of course," he said. "But it never hurts to have a little luck."

Sofia gulped down the rest of her rosé, then lifted her glass, watching the last drops of wine form legs as they ran down the sides.

"Sometimes," she said, "you have to make your own luck."

CHAPTER 22

After the craziness of the last two weeks, the election itself had been something of an anticlimax. In spite of the confusion caused by Chad Chapman's inquiries, enough votes were cast to pass the referendum and Shep was "sworn in" as Fossett's mayor. Even Rod Blakely managed to be a fairly gracious loser. At last, Melanie thought, as she drove back into town, everything she'd worked for was going to pay off. Chad had called her the night before; their story would be on *Weekend Extra* that afternoon at four thirty.

Since Melanie got the good news, there'd been a mad scramble to get the auditorium ready. After years of high hopes and crushing disappointments, she wanted as many people as possible to see what she hoped would be the thing that launched Fossett into a new, more prosperous future. As she pulled up outside the auditorium's double doors, she saw Pete and Walt carrying folding chairs inside. Tagging along after them was Shep, still carrying Mr. Stuffy.

Melanie swallowed, feeling a stab of regret. She wished Bryce could have been there to witness this. Without his help, the election might never have taken place. Looking back on that first town meeting, she couldn't believe how unprepared she'd been for what was to come or how much work would actually be involved. Bryce was right: If you wanted to get results, you had to be willing to do what was hard, not just what was easy. She'd worked hard to make this dream come true, but she'd never have done it without him.

When she walked inside, Walt was hooking up the cable linking the satellite feed to the projector. Installing a dish on the roof had been part of a previous improvement project, but funds had run out before the town had purchased a projector, so when she found out that the show would be on that night Melanie had hurried out to rent one. Unfortunately, when they'd gotten back to Fossett, Walt had found that the bulb inside had burned out, necessitating the trip from which she'd just returned.

He looked up.

"You got it?"

"Right here." She held up two bulbs. "Plus

a spare, just in case."

"Good idea," he said. "We don't want to miss this."

Pete was up on a ladder, checking the electrical plug in the ceiling to make sure the breaker hadn't tripped. Once the projector was mounted, everything they'd need to power it and capture the signal would be right there. Finally having the money to complete the projects she'd begun over the last four years was something else Melanie was looking forward to.

Shep stood at the door, greeting everyone as they came inside. Whether or not he understood the role he'd played in generating this excitement, he did seem to be enjoying it. Other than his meltdown over the pilfered treat on Friday, he'd been more patient and hardworking than anyone could ever have expected, and Melanie was very proud. Mayor or not, however, after the show tonight it would be time to give him a rest.

People were arriving in anticipation, most of them bringing food or drink to share. As Melanie watched the offerings pile up on the stage, she was reminded of why she'd tried so hard to resuscitate her hometown. Fossett might be small, but it had a big heart. Of all the things Bryce had warned her about, that was the one that had worried her the most: Whatever acclaim or popularity it gained from this show, she hoped the heart of Fossett would still be the same.

The auditorium was getting full. She glanced at the clock: sixteen minutes until the show started. Melanie had texted Bryce that morning, giving him a heads-up, but hadn't yet gotten a reply. She took out her phone and checked the status again. It said the text had been delivered, but whether or not he'd actually read it was anyone's guess. She licked her lips and considered giving him a call to make sure he'd gotten the message. No, she thought, there wasn't enough time. Chad had warned Melanie that there was no way of knowing when, during the one-hour broadcast, his piece would run; she couldn't take the chance of missing it. She hurriedly typed in a second message and hit "send." If Bryce missed the show after this, she thought, at least it wouldn't be her fault.

The bulb had been replaced and the projector mounted on the ceiling, the screen above the stage was in place, and Pete was adjusting the angle to make sure the picture would be centered. Everything was in place and ready for the show to start. Walt walked over and stood next to Melanie, the two of them watching as the crowd continued to stream in.

"How you doing?" he whispered.

She gave him a nervous smile.

"Hanging in there. How about you?"

"About the same."

"Looks like the whole town turned out," she said.

"Pretty close. We're missing a few folks from Little Russia, but the Gulins are here. They'll take word back to the rest."

"What about Lou Tsimiak?"

Walt shook his head.

"No, he's up in his tower, still keeping a lookout."

Melanie sighed. She'd been hoping to tell him again how grateful she was that he'd saved Bryce after that hornet sting.

"I hate to see him isolate himself like that," she said. "People around here don't blame him for what happened."

"Maybe not, but he's not doing himself any favors standing up in that tower all day."

"Poor guy. I wonder if he'll ever feel like the war is over. Bryce thinks he's looking for a way to atone for missing that shot."

Walt shrugged and continued scanning the room.

"Did you see Rod?"

She searched the rows of friends and neighbors.

"I must have missed him. Where is he?"

He pointed.

"First row. Smack dab in the middle."

Melanie felt her stomach sink. Of course he was. Probably hoping the whole thing would blow up in her face, too, so he could be right up front to rub it in.

"It's like watching a movie with a film critic in the first row."

Walt nodded toward the clock.

"Well, whether he likes it or not, we'll find out soon enough. Excuse me while I dim the lights."

As the room darkened, the voices in the room turned from boisterous chatter to whispers of anticipation. Pete turned the projector on and began adjusting the focus, leaving the sound muted until the show began. Shep finished his rounds and came over to sit beside her, setting Mr. Stuffy at her feet. Melanie gave him a hug and took out her phone again. Still no reply from Bryce.

"This is going to be fun," she told Shep. "You're going to be a star."

At last the show's logo was splashed across the screen and the theme music came on. There were a few scattered demands to, "turn it up!" from the audience, prompting Pete to make a hasty adjustment to the volume, but by the time the show's impossibly good-looking co-hosts appeared on-screen, the auditorium had fallen silent. Everyone seemed to be holding their breath, waiting and wondering to see what would happen. Then suddenly, a picture of Shep flashed across the screen. A chorus of gasps and excited chatter broke the silence and quickly died away as the host introduced the segment.

"With polls showing that fewer than half of Americans trust their political leaders, perhaps it's no surprise that some folks are willing to take a chance on a different kind of candidate. Tonight, reporter Chad Chapman takes us to a little town in Oregon where an experiment in democracy is taking place."

A brief montage of people yelling across picket lines, arguing on street corners, and punching one another at police rallies filled the screen, accompanied by Chad's voice-over:

"You hear it every day on the news: Americans are tired of politics as usual. But what if there was a candidate that nearly everyone approved of?"

A second picture of Shep, this one of him sitting at his desk in a collar and tie, went up, provoking a chorus of gasps and excited chatter in the audience that quickly died away as the narration continued.

"Meet Shep, a five-year-old border collie who's just been elected mayor of Fossett, Oregon."

Melanie bent down and pointed to the screen.

"Look," she whispered. "That's you up there."

"A dog might seem to be an unlikely choice for mayor," Chad continued, *"but Shep's got plenty of fans. We spoke to a few of them to see what they had to say about their mayor-elect."*

Shep's picture changed to a series of shots of Chad, interviewing members of the community:

A stunned-looking Ernest and Francine Stubbs at their goat ranch:

"Most politicians are all talk, but when our goats get out, Shep's right there to round them up."

Jewell Divine holding forth in her cluttered home:

"Shep has an unusually large amount of compassion for an animal. I sensed it immediately."

A drone hovering over an amused-looking Chad's head:

"I think we'll assume that's a 'no comment.' "

The Griebs sitting in their living room:

"We've known Shep since he first came to Fossett. He's a good dog."

Then a breakaway to a close-up shot of a skeptical-looking Chad.

"But is he, in fact, a good dog?"

Melanie frowned.

"What the heck?"

She glanced at Walt, who shook his head and shrugged.

Up on the screen was another picture of Shep, this one grainy and poorly lit, as he trotted toward a goat pen and unlatched the gate. Then a freeze-frame of Shep's guilty face as the goats streamed out of their pen was stamped with the words, "Collie Confidential."

Melanie gasped.

"What? That's not fair," she hissed. "They asked Shep to do that."

Walt put a finger to his lips.

"Shh. It's okay."

But Chad wasn't finished.

"And is this footage from our hidden-camera evidence of Mayor Shep accepting a bribe?"

A shot of Mae slipping Shep a treat behind Melanie's back provoked some guffaws from the audience.

"Looks like you're busted, Mae."

"Oh, for heaven's sake," Melanie said. "This is ridiculous."

"And like any corrupt politician, Mayor Shep isn't afraid to make his displeasure known when the payoffs are withheld."

Melanie gasped as the destruction resulting from Shep's tantrum splashed across the screen.

"Oh no."

"So, why would a town be willing to vote for such an obviously compromised candidate? Perhaps a few words from Shep's opponent will give us a clue."

Heads craned to get Rod's reaction as his face filled the screen.

"The whole election was rigged. This Shep character's beholden to the dog food lobby. You just wait. Pretty soon, we'll all be eating kibble around here."

"And there you have it," Chad sneered. *"This is Chad Chapman signing off from The Craziest Town in America."*

As the show returned to its co-hosts, Pete turned off the projector and turned on the lights. No one said a word as Melanie stood there, stunned and horrified. Chad Chapman had lied to her. The whole thing was just a setup so he could make a hit piece about Fossett, holding it up to ridicule in front of the entire nation. The way he'd portrayed Shep as some sort of criminal canine made Fossett and its residents look like a bunch of boobs for electing him as their mayor.

Bryce had tried to warn her, she thought, but she wouldn't listen. How, she wondered, would they ever recover?

Rod Blakely jumped to his feet and scrambled onto the stage.

"Did you see that?" he screeched, pointing to the projection screen. "Can you believe it?"

Melanie winced. She could only imagine the sort of criticism she'd be in for now. Whatever he said about her, though, it would be nothing compared to the censure she was already heaping on herself. She took a deep breath. This was her fault. The best thing to do was go up there and apologize, hoping her friends and neighbors didn't run her out of town.

Then Rod threw his hands in the air and cheered.

"We're *famous*!"

At once, everyone was on their feet, cheering, clapping, and giving one another high fives. Melanie stood rooted to the spot. Was it possible this wasn't a disaster after all? She looked over at Walt, who turned his hands up in wonder.

As she stood there, dumbstruck, Melanie heard people in the audience speculating about how best to capitalize on their new-found stardom. Where had all these ideas about business opportunities, branding, and investment strategies come from?

Bryce was right, she thought. There'd always been plenty of talent in Fossett. All it needed was for someone to fan that spark of potential into a flame, and from the looks on everyone's faces, this fire was going to burn more brightly than any of them could have imagined. She'd done it, Melanie thought. Maybe not in the way she'd intended to, but she was the one who'd made it happen. She only wished she hadn't driven Bryce away at the same time. She covered her face with her hands and burst into tears.

"Hey there," Walt said, giving her a hug. "What's wrong?"

Melanie turned and sobbed into his chest.

"Isn't this what you wanted?" He patted her back. "I'd have thought you'd be over-joyed."

"I am, Walt, but look what it cost me.

Bryce will never forgive me."

He gave her a skeptical look.

"Oh, I don't think I'd give up on Bryce just yet, if I were you."

"But the things I said . . ."

"Can't be unsaid — by either of you — I understand that, but that man loves you. Give him a call and tell him you're sorry. I think you'll find he's as sorry as you are."

She sniffled. "You really think so?"

Walt laughed.

"There's only one way to find out."

Melanie bounced onto her tiptoes and kissed his cheek.

"I'll be right back."

CHAPTER 23

Flakes of powdery snow fell as Melanie loaded the projector television into her Honda the next day. She'd decided to return the equipment to the rental place herself rather than ask someone else to do it. The truth was, she and Shep needed a break.

The border collie was already on the back seat, lying on his side as he watched her get into the car. People had been coming into the shop all morning wanting to shake his paw or give treats to the new mayor, and Melanie had decided it would be better to take Shep with her than have him overindulge on their well-intentioned goodies. Heaven forbid he should ever say no.

"If this keeps up, I'll have to put up a sign that says: 'Please Don't Feed the Mayor,' " she told him as she started the car.

It was only a half-hour drive into the city, but the winding roads and snowy conditions slowed them down and it was nearly noon before they pulled up in front of ABC Production Rentals. By that time, Shep was sound asleep and she was loath to wake him. It had been an exciting night for both of them; she was glad at least one of them was able to get some rest. After talking to Bryce, she'd been too keyed up to fall asleep until well after midnight.

Walt had been right to encourage her to call. After their argument on Friday, Bryce told her, he'd been feeling pretty low.

"I was wrong," he said. "I'm sorry."

"No. You were right: I hadn't been listening to anyone else. I think that's why I was so upset when you said I was being selfish. I was so sure that I was right that I was determined to prove it no matter what."

"So what do we do now?"

It was the question she'd been asking herself.

"I guess I don't know," she said. "I mean, things may not have worked out the way I'd expected, but my plan did work. Making Shep the mayor has stirred things up and given people around here the push they needed to try out some of their own ideas. I don't think that'll change if we leave."

"I can't let you do that, Mel. After all you've done I wouldn't feel right depriving

Fossett of its mayor."

She'd nearly broken down then. Melanie had been sure that once the election was over, the two of them could patch things up. Instead, making Shep the mayor had just thrown one more roadblock into their path.

"But if I don't leave, I won't have you," she sobbed. "I'll always care about Fossett, but I love you and I don't want to lose you again. Even Shep doesn't want that."

"You sure about that?"

She'd laughed a little at that.

"Oh yeah. You should see him. He's been carrying Mr. Stuffy around ever since you left."

"Well, maybe there's a way to make us all happy," Bryce said. "I've been doing a lot of thinking in the last forty-eight hours."

"What about?"

"How about we talk about it in person?" he said. "I have a few things to do up here in the morning, but I can head down after that."

"Sounds good," she told him. "I have to drop the projector off at the rental place in Corvallis. How about if I give you a call before I leave?"

Melanie looked up at the storefront. A sign in the window said: No Dogs Al-

LOWED. She glanced back at Shep, who was still snoring softly on the back seat. She was only going to be inside for a minute, she thought. He'd be all right by himself. And the snow was no longer falling. She cracked the windows a few inches so he could get some air, then grabbed the projector and went inside.

The manager stepped out from behind the counter to greet her.

"Hey, it's the TV star!"

Melanie blushed as the only other customer in the store turned to look at her.

"I brought your equipment back," she said, setting it on the counter.

"How did it go?" he asked. "Did everyone get to see the show?"

She smiled.

"Yeah, it went really well. Everybody was excited to see themselves on TV."

"I can imagine. We watched it here in the shop. I kept telling everyone how you'd rented a TV from us just the day before. They all said to tell you how cute your new mayor is."

She glanced back toward the parking lot. From that angle, it was impossible to see her car.

"Speaking of whom," she said. "He's waiting for me in the car, so if you don't mind . . ."

"Oh, sure," the man said. "Hold on, let me get your paperwork."

He reached under the counter and pulled out a cardboard box filled with receipts. Melanie felt herself wilt inside. She'd been hoping to just drop the thing off and run. Now she'd have to stand there and wait while he searched through the papers looking for hers.

"My wife and I were thinking we might drive out to Fossett one of these days and look around," he said as he riffled through the files. "Seemed like it might be a good place to retire."

"Yes," she said, trying not to sound impatient. "Fossett has a lot of things going for it."

The man pulled out a paper from the pile to take a closer look.

"No, that's not it."

Melanie looked around.

"Would you mind if I just step outside a minute to check on my dog?"

"I'll check on him, ma'am."

She turned and smiled at a young man wearing a green vest with the letters *ABC* on the shoulder.

"If you're sure it's not too much trouble."

"Oh, no trouble," the boy said.

As he headed outside, the manager pulled her receipt from the pile.

"Here it is!"

He set it on the counter and handed her a pen.

"If you'd just initial here and sign at the bottom, we'll be done."

Melanie took the pen and signed quickly.

"Thank you so much," she said.

"Good luck," the manager told her. "Maybe we'll see you in town, eh?"

"Sure."

The young man walked back into the store just as she was tucking the receipt in her purse.

"Your dog's just fine," he told her.

"Thank you," Melanie said. "I appreciate your checking on him."

"Oh, it's no problem. Your husband said he could keep an eye on him till you get back."

She looked at him.

"My husband?"

"Yeah. He said he'd wait for you in the car."

Melanie looked at the door and grinned. Was this the surprise Bryce had hinted at last night?

That stinker. He should have told me.

She hurried outside and glanced at the

car. Bryce wasn't in the car. In fact, she didn't see anyone inside. What was going on? She rushed forward, suddenly terrified. What if someone had stolen Shep?

Melanie was in such a panic that she didn't see the man standing in the shadows. As she reached for the car door, he stepped up and grabbed her arm. She felt something cold and hard pressing against her ribs.

"Don't say anything," he said. "Or the dog dies."

CHAPTER 24

They changed drivers at an abandoned gas station a few miles from town. Melanie had been driving for nearly an hour, Colton forcing her to make capricious turns, doubling back on roads already traveled and changing speed erratically in what could only have been evasive maneuvers designed in ensure that they were not being followed. As Melanie stepped out of the car, she felt dizzy and disoriented.

She glanced anxiously into the back seat. Shep still lay, head down, the rope around his neck bunching up the fur behind his ears. His breathing was slow but steady. On the floor below him lay a half-eaten dog treat, the means by which he'd been subdued.

Colton followed her gaze and chuckled.

"I never have known a dog that could resist a treat, even from a stranger. He must have realized there was something wrong after the first swallow, but by then it was too late. Greedy little bastard."

Melanie's heart leaped as Shep's eyes began to flutter.

"I think he's coming around," she said.

"Wouldn't be surprised," he said. "Xanax doesn't last that long — especially if the dosage is low."

He sneered at Shep.

"Don't get any ideas there, doggie. That's a slipknot around your neck: You tug, it tightens. Tug too hard and it'll be lights-out for good."

Melanie clenched her teeth, feeling a surge of impotent fury.

"Why are you doing this to us?"

"Temper, temper," he said. "Don't forget who's running this show."

Colton waved the gun, indicating that she should join him on the other side of the car.

"Do what I say and you might just get out of this alive."

He shoved her into the passenger's seat and slammed the door.

"Now you just sit tight. I need to see a man about a dog."

As Colton walked around the back of the car to relieve himself, laughing at his own joke, Melanie saw her chance. She took out her iPhone and hurriedly dialed 911, then slipped the phone back into her pocket and listened to the phone ring, praying the operator would pick up before Colton got back into the car.

"Nine-one-one. What's your emergency?"

She heard Colton zip his pants. She had only seconds to talk.

"I need help," she whispered. "Please don't hang up."

As the door swung open, Melanie jumped and said a silent prayer that the operator would know not to speak. Colton slid into the driver's seat and started the engine.

"Where are we going?" Melanie said, unnerved by the tremolo in her voice.

"That's for me to know and you to find out."

He put the Honda in gear and peeled out of the parking lot.

She put on her seat belt and closed her eyes. Emergency operators could use cell phone transmissions to triangulate a caller's signal; with her phone number on an open line, they should be able to approximate her location. Of course, they'd be looking for a moving target. If there were some way for her to let them know what was going on, maybe it would improve the chances that law enforcement in the area would find them. She had to say something — anything

— to let the operator know what was happening and where they were going.

Melanie licked her lips, her mouth too dry to swallow.

"Can I ask you something?"

He shrugged.

"Ask away. Doesn't mean I have to answer."

"Are you Jesse Lee Colton?"

Colton grinned.

"Smart girl."

She nodded. At least the authorities would know who they were looking for now. She looked around for any landmarks that might help pinpoint their location.

"We're heading north," she said as casually as she could. "There was a sign back there for I-5. Are we going to Salem?"

"Nope."

"Where, then?"

Colton jerked the wheel to the right, sending dirt and gravel flying as the car went briefly off the tarmac. In the back seat, Shep whimpered as the rope tightened around his neck.

"What are you doing?" she screamed. "You're going to choke him!"

"That's right," he said. "And I'm going to keep doing it until you shut up."

She licked her lips again and pressed her

back into the seat, waiting for Colton to calm down so she could try again. The rope hadn't hurt Shep, she thought, only startled him. As long as he remained on the seat, he'd be okay — a safer bet than having the cops fail to find them. She pulled her feet up and turned her face to the window, hoping Colton would forget about her while she considered her next move.

If he wouldn't tell her where they were going, Melanie thought, perhaps she could say something about the area they were passing through. Landmarks, road conditions — lots of things might be able to give the operator a clue to their location.

"The trees around here have all lost their leaves," she said. "We have mostly evergreens out in Fossett."

"Mmm."

Then, a few minutes later:

"Those hay bales are huge."

He nodded absently.

"I grew up just ten miles from here. That's about thirty miles from —"

"What are you, a goddamned tour guide? I don't need you to tell me where we are."

Melanie shrank back. The violence of the man's outburst was terrifying.

"But maybe," he said, his eyes narrowing, "someone else does."

Without thinking, she rested her hand protectively on the pocket that held her phone.

"What've you got in there?" he said, slapping her hand away. "Lemme see."

Colton wrenched the phone from her pocket and Melanie cried out in dismay.

"Were you making phone calls while I was indisposed? Hoping the cavalry might come and save you?"

Melanie grabbed for the phone.

"Help!"

Colton backhanded her across the face.

"Keep quiet," he snarled as he broke the connection. "They were never going to find you out here, anyway."

Melanie cowered, feeling tears of pain and frustration well up. No one had ever struck her like that before. She put a hand to her cheek and felt the beginnings of a welt start to form.

"What do you mean?"

"Not enough cell towers to triangulate," he said, miming a sad face. "That's what you get for living out in the boonies."

"I don't believe you," she said without conviction.

Then Colton gave her a sly smile.

"But you know," he said. "That's not such a bad idea. Maybe we should call for help."

He opened the Contacts on her phone and started swiping through the names.

"Let's just see who's in here."

As he searched through the list, Colton kept taking his eyes off the road and the Honda began to swerve. He crossed the middle line, overcorrected, and swung onto the right-hand shoulder, raising a cloud of dust behind them. Melanie's heart was in her throat.

"Don't — please," she begged. "Let me do it. Just tell me who you want to call."

She reached for the phone and he jerked it away, yanking the wheel at the same time and taking the Honda back into oncoming traffic. Melanie heard a horn blare and looked up. A semi was coming straight at them, its wheels smoking, its driver laying on the horn as he braked.

"Look out!"

She grabbed the wheel and jinked the car back into its lane just as the truck blew past, so close it made the Honda tremble. As the horn's pitch dropped and then faded in the distance, Melanie realized her entire body was numb. If the truck had hit them, she thought, she'd never have felt a thing. She closed her eyes and prayed she wouldn't regret her decision to stay alive.

Colton, meanwhile, seemed not to have

noticed the danger they'd been in. It was as if escaping death was an everyday occurrence. He pressed a button on the phone and put it to his ear.

Melanie glared at him.

"What are you doing?"

"I told you," he said. "I'm calling for help."

Help for whom? she wondered. Not for himself, surely. Bryce had told her that Colton preferred to watch his victims die, to see them up close as they took their last breath. That's why shooting Vance had been so out of character. Colton had promised to kill his prosecutors in the same way he'd murdered his other victims.

As the answer finally dawned, it filled her with horror. Melanie shook her head.

No, no, no. Not Bryce. Please. Don't call Bryce.

"Oh, dear," Colton said. "Looks like I'll have to leave a message."

He winked at her just as Melanie heard a muffled beep.

"Hey, MacDonald. I think you know who this is. I've got your little lady friend with me and we're heading back to her place. Meet us there in an hour if you want to see her alive again. Oh, and please don't call the authorities. This is just between you and me."

Colton hung up.

"There," he said. "That should do it."

Melanie looked away, wondering which of Bryce's numbers he'd called. If it was his cell, there was a chance that he wouldn't check his messages in time to meet them in Fossett. She hoped he wouldn't. She didn't want him to put himself in jeopardy, and even if her phone wasn't turned on, she thought there was still a chance that the authorities would be able to locate it. The longer Colton was kept waiting for Bryce, the better the chances that the police would show up in time to save her.

A blast of frigid air swept through the car, sending bits of paper flying as the driver's side window came down. Melanie reached up, trying to keep her hair out of her eyes.

"What are you doing?"

"Leading the hounds astray."

He pulled back his arm and threw her phone across the road. It skittered briefly along the shoulder, then tumbled down the embankment on the other side. As Melanie watched it disappear from view, it felt as if her hopes were being carried right down with it.

"I thought you said no one could track us out here," she said.

"Yeah, well," he said. "You can't be too careful, can you?"

CHAPTER 25

Preston Daniels stared at the piece of paper for several minutes before saying anything. When he finally set the resignation letter aside, he seemed perplexed. He pursed his lips and frowned.

"I don't understand, Bryce," he said. "You've done a great job for us this last year. I thought you were enjoying it here at Norcross Daniels."

"Thank you, sir. I've learned a lot here and I'll always think of my time at this firm with fondness."

"But you're still going to leave."

"Yes."

The old man frowned and steepled his fingers.

"If it's the money, you should know that year-end bonuses will be quite substantial."

"It's not the money, sir, believe me. The compensation package has been more than generous."

Daniels glanced at the letter again.

"It wouldn't have anything to do with Judge Cardoza, would it? She did ask for you, but I could reassign —"

"No, sir. It has nothing to do with her."

Bryce kept his gaze steady. The fact was, Sofia Cardoza had had a lot to do with his resignation. But not for the reason Daniels was implying.

"It's simply time for me to move on."

For the first time since Bryce had walked into his office, the senior partner seemed perturbed.

"You do remember the noncompete clause in your contract."

"I assure you, I won't be violating it in my new position."

Daniels sighed.

"Well then, I suppose there's nothing else for me to do but say good-bye."

The two men stood and shook each other's hands.

"Best of luck, Bryce. For your sake, I hope you won't regret leaving us."

"I don't think I will, sir, but thank you."

Bryce walked back to his office and grabbed his things, taking one last look around his office. Working at Norcross Daniels had been a great opportunity, one he'd never forget, but he'd finally realized that his heart simply wasn't in it.

He had Sofia to thank for that. Her disregard for the character of her clients and her willingness to do anything to win their cases were what made her a great defender, but they were also the things that Bryce could never adopt in good conscience. He'd been so desperate to get out of debt and so flattered that Daniels would hire him that he'd let it blind him to his own principles. Asa was right, he thought. Bryce wasn't cut out to be a defender.

He closed his office door and headed straight for the parking garage, noting that the homeless man who usually sat outside wasn't there that day. As he got into his car and pulled out into traffic, the thought occurred to him that the man might have been the one the police had found stabbed in his sleeping bag the week before. The bigger Portland grew, it seemed, the more people there were falling through the cracks. Just one more reason to leave, as far as he was concerned.

As he got on the freeway, Bryce started rehearsing what he would say to Melanie. It wasn't that Fossett had suddenly become a more promising place for him to practice law; it was that he'd finally realized that the things it did have outweighed any sacrifice he'd have to make to live there. Corvallis wasn't that far away, Salem less than an hour, and Glen Wheatley had told him there was a good chance that one or the other would hire him. If Bryce returned to the DA's office, he'd be doing what he loved for a living and living with the person he loved. All he had to do now was convince Melanie that it was worth taking the risk.

He stopped for gas in Salem and gave her a call to let her know he was coming. Bryce had tried to contact her before he left town, but there was no answer at Ground Central and he'd been anxious to get on the road. A week ago, he would have been surprised that no one had answered, but with the town still celebrating their star turn on *Weekend Extra,* perhaps she'd decided to take a break and enjoy the run. No doubt, there'd be plenty of calls from reporters wanting to interview her now. He wondered if Dave Giusti was regretting his decision.

Bryce was about to try Melanie's cell number when he saw that he'd gotten a message from her. He hit the playback and waited to hear what she had to say.

"Hey, MacDonald. I think you know who this is."

Colton's voice was like a stab to the heart. What was he doing with Melanie's phone?

As the obvious answer came to him, Bryce closed his eyes and tried to calm the panic that was welling up inside. Where had she been when he'd spoken to her last? At an equipment rental place, somewhere in Corvallis. She told him she was heading home. Nothing had indicated that she was in trouble.

"I've got your little lady friend with me and we're heading back to her place."

Imagining Melanie under the control of that pitiless butcher, Bryce had to fight the urge to retch. Running into her couldn't have been an accident, he thought; the man obviously knew who she was. Somehow, he must have connected her to Bryce, but how? It wasn't as if Colton could have seen the two of them together; he'd have had to recognize her car.

The Honda. Bryce had driven it to work when his car was being detailed. Colton must have seen him in it and used his contacts to find out where she lived. Finding her in Corvallis would have taken luck on his part, but it wasn't impossible. Colton might even have followed her awhile, hoping she'd lead him to Bryce. The thought made him ill. He'd thought that having Jesse Lee Colton find him was the worst thing that could happen, but this was much, much worse.

Oh, Mel. What have I done to you?

The attendant knocked on his window and Bryce handed him his card before playing the message again. Without the initial shock of hearing Colton's voice, he was able to listen to it dispassionately, feeling his fear and anger turn to a steely resolve. By the time the message was over, he knew what he had to do. Colton was right. This situation had nothing to do with Melanie. To fix it, he'd have to face the man alone.

The message said he had an hour to get to Melanie's place, a forty-minute drive from there. Bryce checked the time stamp; it had been left only nine minutes before. He'd be cutting it close.

Colton had told him not to contact the authorities, but that didn't mean he couldn't alert anyone else to the situation. Bryce had no way of knowing how far the two of them had been from Fossett when the message was left; for all he knew, they were already at Melanie's house, waiting for him. Bryce might be the one Colton was after, but that didn't mean the man wouldn't threaten anyone else who got in his way. The people in town needed to know what was going on, and there was only one person he knew who could get the word out without causing a panic. He dialed the number and put it on speaker, then started his car and peeled out of the parking lot. It took five rings before anyone picked up.

"Gunderson's."

"Hey, Walt, it's Bryce MacDonald. I need your help."

As the car pulled into her driveway, Melanie's eyes filled with tears. Shep had woken up a few minutes before, but a few tugs at the rope had convinced him that escape wasn't an option and he'd quickly abandoned the effort. Colton had been so absorbed in trying to negotiate the twists and turns of the road leading into town that he hadn't bothered to stop her from uttering a few soothing words to keep the collie calm. She'd been careful not to say too much, though. There was no sense in aggravating a man with a gun.

Colton shut off the engine and checked his watch.

"Twelve more minutes," he said. "Let's hope your sweetheart is on time. Otherwise —" He lifted the gun and mimed shooting her.

Melanie cringed. The thought of having a bullet tear through her body was terrifying, but it didn't keep her from hoping that Bryce wouldn't make it on time. There was no reason to think that Colton would let her go even if he did, and the last thing she wanted was for both of them to be in her position. If he'd heard the message at all, she hoped that Bryce had called the police. In the meantime, though, she was going to do whatever it took to keep her captor calm.

"Would you like to come in?" she said, trying to show a graciousness she didn't feel.

Colton grinned.

"Ooh, such hospitality. You going to offer me something to drink, too? Maybe put out a couple of cookies while you're at it?"

She nodded stiffly.

"If you'd like."

He scratched his cheek with the gun barrel as he considered her offer.

"That does sound good, now you mention it. Less chance of being seen, too." He nodded. "Let's go."

Melanie motioned toward the back seat.

"And my dog? Can he come in, too? He might be thirsty."

Colton looked around at Shep.

"All right," he said. "As long as he minds his manners."

He glared at the dog.

"You act up, though, doggie, and it's all

over, understand?"

Melanie nodded at Shep.

"You'll be good, won't you?"

Shep's gaze switched from Melanie to Colton and back. He thumped his tail one time.

"That means yes," she said, not really knowing if it was true.

As Colton opened his door, Shep looked at her and thumped his tail a second time as if trying to reassure her. Melanie bit her lip, trying to hold back tears.

"You stay there," she whispered. "I'll come around and get you."

The neighborhood was quiet — almost eerily so — as Melanie stepped out of the car. One thing she'd always appreciated about life in Fossett was that the neighbors kept an eye on one another — a big plus for a woman living alone. Long hours at her shop hadn't kept her from making friends with the people who lived around her, either; they'd notice anything suspicious or out of the ordinary. Mrs. Scudder from next door should have been peering out from behind her lace curtains by now, yet there was no face in the window, and Luke Mears across the way had left the fence he was working on half-done. She didn't know whether she should be alarmed or relieved, but at least their absence would save her from having to wave them off.

"Hey, give a hand here."

Colton was standing next to the car, his gun trained on Shep. The collie hadn't moved from his place on the back seat, but he was baring his teeth, making it clear that he would protect his mistress if given the chance. Melanie hurried over and stepped between the two of them, turning her back on the gun as she reached in to untie the rope that bound her dog to the door handles.

"It's okay," she said, tugging the knots apart. "He won't bite you if I'm here, will you, Shep?"

Colton hunched his shoulders and glanced around nervously.

"Hurry it up. I don't like being exposed like this."

Melanie felt her temper flare.

Maybe if you hadn't tied him so tightly I could.

"Don't worry," she said, trying to sound cheerful. "If anyone was home around here, they'd have poked their heads out by now. They've probably all gone into town."

Melanie gave the dog's neck a quick check as she pulled the rope free, then tied it around his collar so she could take him inside. Shep was an obedient animal, but they'd never been in a situation like that; she didn't trust him not to make a lunge for their tormentor. She couldn't blame him, but neither did she want Colton to do something drastic. A man who could murder people in cold blood, after all, would think nothing of killing a dog.

She and Shep led the way into the house. As Melanie stepped inside, she felt her senses heighten. It was as if she were seeing the place for the first time. Every piece of furniture, every picture, every memento, evoked a feeling of tenderness that was almost painful. This was the life she'd made for herself, something strong and sturdy, yet now that it was threatened, it all seemed so fragile. More than that, she realized how empty it was. In trying to make a life that was all her own, she'd become solitary, cutting herself off from the possibility of real intimacy. What did any of it mean if she had no one to share it with?

She closed her eyes and imagined she was sending her thoughts to Bryce.

Please don't come. I don't want to lose you.

"You got a leash for that dog?"

Melanie nodded.

"In the kitchen. I'll get it."

"I'll go with you," he said. "You still owe

me that drink, remember?"

Shep kept his head down as they walked into the kitchen. Through the rope, Melanie could feel his throat vibrating with a growl too quiet to hear, and she was anxious to put on his leash. As she took it off the hook, she made a lowering motion with her hand and the dog reluctantly lay down. If she saw an opportunity to make a move against Colton, they'd do it together, but right now was no time for heroics. She snapped the lead on to his collar and held out the rope. Colton snatched it out of her hand and started pawing through her kitchen drawers, keeping the gun pointed toward her.

At last, he found what he was looking for. As Colton took out the knife, Melanie gasped. Was he going to carve her up the way he'd done to his other victims?

Instead, the man used the knife to slice the rope in half, then stuck the looped pieces into his belt.

"So," he said, looking around. "What've you got?"

Melanie kept Shep on a short lead as she walked toward the refrigerator. Her legs felt as stiff and heavy as greenwood logs.

"I have iced tea and lemonade," she said. "Also milk —"

"Milk? Jesus, who do you think you're

talking to? How about a beer?"

She shook her head.

"I don't have any. There's half a bottle of wine, if you'd like that."

He made a face.

"Better than nothing," he said. "Hand it over."

Melanie looked at the bottle.

"Don't you want a glass?"

The man laughed.

"No, I'm good," he said, taking it from her hand. "Wouldn't want to trouble you any."

Melanie looked around. Coming home had released some of the tension she'd felt the last hour and a half, leaving her drained and exhausted.

"Would you mind if I sit down?"

Colton had already chugged most of the wine. He lowered the bottle and pointed it toward the living room.

"Let's go up front where I can keep an eye on things. MacDonald should be here soon," he said, then added with a grin: "If you're lucky."

Melanie gave Shep's lead a tug and they led the way back to the front room, where she took him to his bed and told him to lie down.

"I'd better stay with my dog," she said.

"There's no place to tie him up over here."

Colton narrowed his eyes skeptically, but he'd seen how tightly she'd been holding the collie's lead. Even with a gun in his hand, the thought of facing a snarling, charging animal must have given him pause.

"All right," he said. "But don't try anything. One wrong move and I'll shoot you both."

Shep took longer than usual to find the right spot to settle down. He kept circling his bed, whining softly as he nudged Mr. Stuffy closer, then slowly lowered his haunches and set his head on top of the little felt and yarn doll. Melanie looked away and a tear ran down her cheek.

He must be thinking about Bryce.

As they sat there listening to the seconds tick by, Melanie noticed once again how quiet the world outside seemed. Where was everyone? She glanced at the clock and realized the time was almost up. If the hour passed without any sign of Bryce, what would Colton do? Change his mind? Grant her a reprieve? Or just kill her where she sat? No matter what he had in mind, she'd find out soon enough.

Shep lifted his head, whimpering softly, and Melanie tightened her grip on the leash. Had he sensed someone out there? She hadn't heard a car. Maybe one of her neighbors had decided to stop by for a visit. Then Bryce's voice shattered the stillness of the quiet street.

"I'm here, Colton! Come on out so we can talk."

The fugitive scuttled across the room, staying to one side as he peered out the window.

"Well, well," he said. "Look who's here."

He glanced at his watch.

"And just in time, too."

He pointed the gun at Melanie.

"Tie the dog to that table leg and get over here."

She led Shep to the dining room and secured his leash to one of the heavy oaken legs, then walked over to the window. Colton was crouched, scanning the area for anyone other than Bryce.

"The place looks deserted. Where is everybody?" he said.

She shrugged.

"I told you, they probably went into town."

He lunged, grabbing her arm, and pointed the gun at her face. Melanie winced and turned away.

"You'd better hope that's true," he said. "If this is a trick, you're going to be sorry."

He twisted her arm behind her back and forced her toward the door. Melanie's heart hammered in her chest as she stumbled forward.

"Open it — just enough so I can see out over you."

She did as she was told.

Bryce was standing at the curb. At the sight of him, Melanie sobbed in relief. He looked as if he'd run there: His face was flushed and his hair had tumbled into his eyes. She'd never been happier to see him, or more sorry. Why hadn't he just called the police?

Colton pulled her closer, pressing himself against her back as he stepped up to the door. The rank smell of body odor turned her stomach. She could feel his breath in her hair.

"Where's your car?" he shouted.

"About ten miles back. I ran out of gas."

"How'd you get here?"

Bryce put out his thumb — the international symbol for hitching a ride.

Colton snickered. The thought of a man hitchhiking in a suit and tie must have amused him.

"Idiot."

Melanie had been trying without success to catch Bryce's eye. Now he looked directly at her and smiled.

"Let the girl and her dog go," he said. "You said it yourself, Colton: This is between you and me."

The man's grip tightened as he drew her closer to him.

"Know what?" he said. "I think maybe I'll just keep her. Been a long time since I had a woman."

Melanie felt her knees weaken. *Of course,* she thought. Colton had never intended to let her go. He'd merely used her to lure Bryce there so he could kill him and do whatever he wanted to with her. The thought was horrifying, but she couldn't see a way out. With a gun in his hand, the man could do whatever he pleased; there was no one around to stop him.

Then something moved on the other side of the street. The door to Luke's house opened and Walt Gunderson stepped out.

"Maybe you ought to think again!" he shouted.

Colton nudged the door just wide enough to point his gun at Bryce.

"What is this? I said no tricks."

Walt stepped off the curb, walking slowly toward the house.

"No trick," he said, his voice firm. "I'm just here to take the girl."

"Oh yeah? Then maybe I ought to just shoot you, too."

"You could," Walt said. "But you'd have an awful lot of witnesses."

Suddenly, curtains up and down the street came open and the faces of Melanie's friends and neighbors appeared in the windows. Tears of gratitude and hope filled her eyes. She felt a shove and stumbled onto the porch, followed closely by Colton, who placed the gun against her head.

"Anybody moves and she dies."

"No one's trying to stop you," Bryce said. "I came here like you asked; now you let her go."

He looked at Melanie.

"Where's Shep?"

She gasped as Colton pressed the gun hard against her temple.

"In the dining room," she said. "Tied to the table leg."

Bryce looked back at Walt, who nodded curtly.

"How about we make a trade?" he said. "Straight across — me for her."

"And how's that going to work?" Colton said. "I just let her go and your sharpshooters use my back for a target?"

"Nobody here is armed," Walt said as he took another step.

Melanie cried out as her arm was wrenched backward.

Colton was breathing hard.

"Get back! All of you!"

Bryce had raised his hands in a show of surrender.

"Hey, hey. Take it easy," he said. "It's an exchange, see? You bring her over here and take me instead. Then the two of us can leave these people in peace."

Melanie could hear Colton's teeth grinding as he made up his mind.

"What about the cops?"

"We haven't called the cops," Walt said.

Several seconds went by as he thought about that. Melanie looked pleadingly at Bryce. He glanced at her briefly and shook his head.

"Just like that?" Colton said.

He nodded. "Just like that."

"All right," he said, looking at Walt. "But if any of you makes a move, these two are dead."

Walt nodded. "Understood."

Colton gave Melanie a push and the two of them started forward. As they walked toward Bryce, her eyes were locked on his.

"Here," Colton said, handing her the rope. "Tie his hands together."

Bryce stuck his hands out in front of him,

wrists together.

"Nice try," the man said. "Behind your back, if you please."

He looked at Melanie.

"Make sure it's good and tight."

She looked at Bryce.

"You don't have to do this," she told him tearfully.

He shook his head.

"Don't worry. It'll be all right."

When she'd tied Bryce's hands, Colton ordered him into the car and told her to tie his feet. Melanie was crying so hard, she could barely see what she was doing. Colton grabbed her arm and slammed the door, then shoved her forward. Melanie staggered, stumbled, and fell into Walt's waiting arms.

"I got you," he said, drawing her to him. "It's okay now. Everything's gonna be all right."

He put his arm around Melanie's shoulders and began ushering her away. As they stepped across the street, she looked back and saw Colton get into her car.

"We can't let them go," she said. "We've got to do something, Walt."

"We are doing something," he said. "We're getting you away from that monster."

Melanie tried to shrug him off, but Walt's grip was strong. As he steered her into

Luke's yard, she began to struggle in earnest.

"Let me go," she said, feeling his grip tighten. "If we let him take Bryce away, he'll kill him."

"Keep your britches on. We'll talk about it inside."

The fight seemed to leave her then as everything that had happened since she'd left home that day caught up with her. Melanie sagged and almost lost her footing. Against Walt's determined guidance, she had no choice but to be propelled up Luke's walkway toward his open door. As they stepped inside, she burst into tears, heavy sobs that wracked her body.

Then the door closed behind them and Walt was shaking her by the shoulders. The change in him was so fierce, so unexpected, that Melanie stopped crying.

"Listen to me," he said. "No one's given up on Bryce. The minute he stepped across the road, I called the police."

Melanie sniffed and wiped her face with the back of her hand.

"But you told Colton you hadn't."

He gave her an incredulous look.

"Are you gonna scold me now for lying to a felon?"

"No," she said. "But we can't just sit here.

We have to think of something."

"What do you think we've been doing for the last half an hour?"

"What?" She shook her head. "Who's 'we'?"

"Me, Bryce, everybody."

He waved his arm to indicate the entire town.

"When he got Colton's message, Bryce called me at the store so that we could come up with a plan. He wanted to make sure that you and Shep *and* Fossett would be okay."

Melanie swallowed, remembering how quiet the town had seemed when they drove in. That's why her friends and neighbors had been there to show their faces when Colton threatened to keep her hostage. Bryce had told them what was coming.

"Was letting Colton take him away part of the plan?"

Walt sighed and shook his head.

"We'd been hoping to keep him here until the police arrived, but the dispatcher said the closest units had been following up on a lead about your cell phone."

She nodded.

"Colton threw it out of the car."

"How far away were you?"

Melanie shook her head.

"I'm not sure. Ten miles? Maybe a bit more? We'd been driving a lot of back roads; I'm not sure where we were."

Walt sucked his lips for a moment and pushed them out in a puff of air.

"With the weather like this, that could take twenty minutes or more."

"Will your plan still work if it takes that long?"

He rubbed the back of his neck, looking doubtful.

"I don't know, Mel. We put up a few roadblocks to try and slow him down, and even if they get past those, there's still a ways to go till they get to the freeway. The police should be able to cut them off before they get there."

A cold certainty settled in the pit of Melanie's stomach as she remembered what Bryce had told her about the way Colton had murdered his victims and the threat he'd made against the prosecutors. It wasn't just the kill that he was after; it was everything that came before.

"It won't work," she said. "They're not headed for the freeway."

"Sure they are. It's the only way out of town."

"Colton doesn't care about that. He told Bryce he was going to kill him the same way

328

he did his other victims."

"Meaning what?"

"Meaning we have to stop him before he gets out of town," she said. "Otherwise, he'll take one of the old logging roads into the woods and we'll never find them."

Walt ran a hand down his face.

"Oh, my god."

Outside, a car's engine turned over and tires squealed. They ran to the window and saw the Honda fly down the street with Colton at the wheel. Melanie's mind was racing.

"Where's the first roadblock?"

"Third; then there's another one at Cedar. Those should add another three or four minutes to his time."

"Not enough," Melanie said. "We have to stop them from getting to the end of Main Street. After that, all they'll have to do is take one of the logging roads into the woods and we'll never see them again."

Walt lifted his shoulders and let them fall. He looked utterly defeated.

"I'm sorry, Mel. I just can't think of any other way to slow them down."

Melanie closed her eyes, desperately searching for some way to stop Colton from leaving town. What could stop a car without hurting the people inside?

Of course.

She turned and ran to the front door.

"Where are you going?"

"I'll tell you on the way," she said. "Come on!"

Melanie ran across the street and burst through her front door. Shep was on his feet, his face eager as she dashed through into the dining room and removed his collar.

"Come on, boy. We've got to save Bryce."

People had begun stepping out of their homes to get a better look as Melanie and her dog ran back outside. Walt hurried over to see what was up.

"I know how to slow them down," she said.

"How can we? They're already halfway to Main Street. There isn't any time."

"Not for us," she said. "Not in a car, but Shep can do it."

She looked down and met the collie's gaze.

"Fetch the goats, boy. You understand? Fetch the goats."

She pointed in the direction of the Stubbses' goat ranch.

"Away to me, Shep."

At her signal, the border collie bounded across the street, cutting through Luke's yard as he made a beeline for the far side of town.

"Come on," Melanie said. "Let's go!"

The two men hesitated, looking bewildered. Shep had already made it across the next street and was running flat out. Melanie was losing patience.

"Come *on!*"

Walt and Luke shared a doubtful look.

"What's he going to do with the goats?" Luke said.

"He's going to let them out of their pen."

She was across the street, motioning for Walt and Luke to join her.

"Hurry up or I'll leave you both here!"

Reluctantly, the two men started running. Already, Shep was barely visible in the distance.

"Why'd you do that?" Walt said as the three of them crashed through Luke's backyard. "Those stupid goats'll run right out onto Main Street."

"I know," Melanie said, picking up speed. "I'm counting on it."

CHAPTER 26

The ride out of town was agony. With his hands bound behind his back, Bryce had no way of keeping himself steady as the Honda careened through Melanie's neighborhood. No sooner would he get his feet braced than the car would turn sharply, bashing his head against the window, or brake suddenly, throwing him to the floor. It felt like he'd been tossed into a clothes dryer. Nevertheless, the second Colton had taken out the rope Bryce knew he had a chance.

It wouldn't be easy. His attempt to have his hands tied in front of him had been brushed off with a laugh, as had his plea for Colton to leave his feet unbound. The man had, however, made three crucial mistakes that Bryce could use to his advantage.

The first was cutting the rope in half. With less length in which to tie the knots, Melanie had had to make fewer turns around

Bryce's wrists and legs. The second was not watching how Bryce held his body as he was bound. Colton had made sure she'd tie the ropes tightly, but by subtly maneuvering his wrists and ankles Bryce had been able to give himself enough room within the bindings to work his hands and feet free. And the third mistake had been letting Bryce determine his position in the car. With his upper body behind Colton's line of sight, his efforts to free himself could go undetected. The only thing Bryce hadn't been able to do was give himself more time. For that, the rest of their plan would have to work.

When Bryce called him, Walt had known just what to do. Not only did he have the authority to get everyone in town mobilized, but his knowledge of the people and personalities in town had made it possible for him to tell Bryce what assets he'd have to set a plan in motion. From the moment he'd heard Colton's message, Bryce knew that Melanie and Shep weren't the only ones in peril; once they arrived in Fossett, everyone in town would be at risk. Colton had been waiting almost two years to get his revenge on Bryce, and anyone who got in his way would be taken down with him. It was why Bryce had insisted that no one call the police before Melanie was released or try to interfere once he was in Colton's hands. Trying to shoot a fleeing car was a waste of bullets and picking off a man holding hostages was something even the professionals tried to avoid. It was the only demand Bryce had made when he called from the gas station, and Walt had been as good as his word. Everyone in town had been given a choice: help or hide, but don't hinder.

Being thrown around in the back of a car was making it hard to concentrate, and the rope around his wrists wasn't yielding as quickly as Bryce had hoped. If he couldn't get his hands free, he had to at least get them in front of him. At the very least, he might be able to get his arms around Colton's neck and choke him. It was risky. The seat back would make it difficult to get a clear shot and the man still had a gun, but at least it would slow them down, giving the police more time to arrive.

They were nearing the final turn out of Melanie's neighborhood — a hairpin to the right — and Colton wasn't slowing down. As he turned the wheel, the car lost traction, slid into the curb, and jounced onto the sidewalk. Bryce cried out as his head hit the door, snapping his neck forward. For a moment, he saw stars.

Colton was cackling in the front seat. "Isn't this fun? Whee!"

With the warren-like neighborhood streets behind them, the Honda was picking up speed; Bryce could no longer afford to be cagey. If Colton drove him into the woods, it wouldn't matter that help was almost there. Better to take his chances now and be shot than get carved up like a Thanksgiving turkey. He set his feet against the door, pushed himself upright, and brought his knees to his chest, turning onto his side so he could maneuver his hands under his rear. As his cheek pressed against the window, the heat from his face made a halo of fog on the cold glass. He saw movement out of the corner of his eye: a blur of black and white traveling along a parallel course.

Shep!

Had Colton seen him? Bryce glanced at the rearview mirror. The man seemed oblivious, his eyes focused on the road ahead. Bryce looked out again. What was the collie doing? With a sick feeling, he wondered if the dog was going to try to stop the car. He prayed that wouldn't happen. Colton wouldn't think twice about running over a dog. Then he realized that Shep wouldn't have left Melanie's side unless she'd told him to. What on earth was she thinking?

He'd gotten one leg through his arms by the time they reached the roadblock at the entrance to Third Street. As Colton hit the brakes, Bryce tumbled off the seat and drove a knee into his solar plexus, a blow that left him gasping for air.

"What the hell?"

Colton smacked his hands down on the wheel.

"Did you know about this?"

Bryce cringed, waiting for the man to discover what he'd done and put a bullet in his back. Instead, Colton put the car in neutral and gunned the engine.

"Amateurs," he growled as he slammed it into first.

The car surged forward and the sound of shearing metal pierced the air as the Honda squeezed through a gap between the building on the right and the earthmover that Helena Haas had wrangled into the street. As the car made it through and sped off again, Bryce despaired. He'd been counting on Colton to go around the roadblock, something that would have added at least a minute to the time it took them to reach Main Street. Instead, it had cost him only a few seconds. For the first time since getting into the car, Bryce feared that the plan would fail.

They were less than a block from Main. As they passed First Street, Bryce lifted his head, looking for any sign of Shep. After being held captive so long, the collie might simply have panicked and run off, he thought, though it seemed unlikely. Wherever the dog was going, Bryce was just happy that — so far, at least — Shep hadn't run in front of the car.

The Honda turned left and headed east on Main, the wheels smoking as they skidded through the turn. The city limits were in sight. If he was going to get out of this alive, Bryce had to hurry and make his move.

As the car settled, he brought his right knee up, leaned forward, and slipped his hands around the other leg. With his hands in front of him, Bryce felt a new surge of hope. He kicked off his shoes and began working his right foot free, praying for anything that would give him a few more seconds to free himself. Melanie's tires were nearly bald, he thought. Maybe they'd get a flat.

Then Colton let up on the gas.

"What the —"

As the car slowed, Bryce looked up. Dozens of goats were pouring into the street from the Stubbses' ranch. Romping and leaping, they filled the road, leaving no room for the car to pass.

Colton screamed in frustration.

"Get out of the way!"

He put his hand on the steering wheel and pushed. As the horn blared, the goats stiffened and fell like dominos onto the road in front of them. Not realizing what he'd done, Colton continued to lay on the horn.

"No, no! Stop that!"

As more goats ran into the road and were startled by the horn, they fainted and fell in fright. Colton's face became a mask of rage. He seemed unable or unwilling to stop honking at them.

"Fine," he said, jerking the wheel. "If that's the way you want to die, it's no fault of mine."

The car began to move forward, but slowly, as if something was blocking the way. At first, Bryce wondered if they might have hit a pothole, but when the front end finally collapsed, he realized that the front axle had broken.

By that time, however, his feet were free; seconds later, his hands, too, were unbound. As Colton tried to put the car into reverse, Bryce grabbed for the gun. Colton saw him coming and grabbed the weapon in time to hit him in the face, but the blow loosened his grip and the gun fell onto the floor. With the car disabled and the weapon out of reach, Bryce decided to make a break for it. He kicked the door open and ran.

Shep was on the far side of the road. As Bryce scrambled toward him, the dog barked a greeting that sent three of the recovering goats tumbling back onto the ground.

"Come on, boy," Bryce said. "Let's get out of here. Go!"

The collie turned and ran toward the Stubbses' yard. Bryce heard a pop and saw a spray of gravel fly up ahead of him. Then a second pop and a third. Shep stumbled and fell.

"No!"

Bryce ran forward and fell to his knees, shielding the collie's body with his own. He heard footsteps behind him; saw Colton's shadow on the ground, his arm out-stretched; in the distance, he heard the faint sound of a siren that would arrive too late.

He heard a gunshot and tensed, waiting for the impact of metal on bone. Instead, a scream of rage and pain rent the air. Bryce turned and saw Colton clutching what was left of his right hand, blood dripping through his fingers.

"What the *hell*?" He crouched protectively, scanning the area for the source of the bullet.

"Give yourself up, Colton," Bryce said. "The car's dead and the cops are almost here. You'll never make it."

The man shuddered and tucked the injured hand under his arm.

"You think so?" Colton sneered. "Just watch me."

He turned and ran into the Stubbses' yard, toward Everett's truck. The one with the key fob inside. The one that didn't need a security system.

"This isn't over," he snarled, grabbing the door handle.

"It's too late," Bryce said. "The cops are almost here. Give yourself up."

"Forget it. I'm not going back to jail."

Colton hoisted himself into the front seat.

"I will be back," he said. "You can count on it."

As the truck door slammed and the engine started, Bryce looked down at Shep and smiled.

"Sit up, you little faker. This is going to be good."

CHAPTER 27

Melanie had just passed First Street when she heard the gunshot. Finding the remains of their roadblock on Third had taken the wind out of Walt's sails and he'd insisted she go on without him, promising to catch up once he recovered. Now, tired and winded herself, she staggered toward Main Street, wondering what she would find. Had Shep understood her command? Or had he merely run off to escape danger?

At the intersection, she turned left and her heart leaped. Two blocks away, the street was full of goats. Half of them were lying stiff legged in the road; of the rest, most were already leaping, kicking, and butting heads while the others kept a wary eye out for the dog who'd driven them from their pen. Her Honda had been abandoned, the left front wheel broken against the curb, the front end collapsed on the sidewalk. She felt a surge of triumph — her plan had worked! — followed by a wave of panic as she realized that neither Shep nor Bryce was in sight. She heard someone shouting in the distance and hurried forward to see what was going on.

At first, Melanie couldn't make sense of the scene in front of her. Twenty feet away, she saw Bryce on his knees, crouched protectively over Shep, who lay in front of him. Behind them, Jesse Lee Colton was clutching his right hand, howling in pain as blood pooled on the ground in front of him, the gun he'd been carrying nowhere in sight. He'd obviously been injured, but how? Had Shep attacked him and gotten himself shot? The thought that her dog might have been killed for obeying her command sent a wave of nausea and self-reproach crashing over her.

But if Colton had shot Shep, then where was the gun? Had it blown up? The man looked like he'd lost half his hand. Melanie couldn't think of anything else that would leave the man so grievously injured.

Unless someone else had shot him.

She saw Bryce turn and say something to Colton and Melanie's heart leaped as she saw Shep raise his head. He might be injured, she thought, but at least he was alive. Colton was screaming obscenities, vowing revenge, but without his weapon, the man's threats were meaningless. He turned and ran toward the Stubbses' ranch, still clutching his damaged hand. Melanie watched Bryce bend forward and say something to Shep, and her heart swelled in gratitude as the collie sat up and the two of them turned to watch the man dashing toward Everett's pickup truck.

"Uh-oh," Melanie said, feeling a bubble of nervous laughter rise up in her throat. "Horrible Harry."

Colton had reached the truck, guessing rightly that a workingman's truck in a rural area would most likely have the keys inside, ready to go. Tucking his injured hand under his arm, he yanked the door open and jumped inside, issuing a final threat before slamming the door. As the engine roared to life, Bryce and Shep scrambled to their feet, running past the still-frozen goats to take shelter behind the abandoned car. Melanie ran over, dropped down beside them, and hugged them both.

"Thank God you're safe," she said. "I was so scared you'd be gone before the police arrived."

"It was Shep," Bryce said, hugging the collie's neck. "You should have seen Colton's face when those goats started to fall."

They heard gravel flying and ducked as Colton slammed the Stubbses' truck into gear and peeled out onto the road. Melanie giggled as she watched him go.

"How far do you think he'll get?"

"Good question," Bryce said. "Depends on how sound a sleeper Harry is."

They didn't have long to wait. The truck had just started picking up speed when it began to swerve violently, the cab's interior a blur of waving arms and beating wings. The tires skidded, the door flew open, and Colton tumbled into the road, trying to shake off the rooster that had sunk his talons into the man's back. The sound of police sirens, which had been growing steadily louder, became deafening as three police cars, their blue and white lights flashing, screeched to a halt. Six doors flew open, behind each an officer with a gun, every one of them pointed at the man on the ground. Oblivious to the danger, and having successfully defended his territory, Harry hopped off Colton's back and returned to his mobile coop. The grateful fugitive put his still-bleeding hands behind his head and was quickly surrounded and taken into custody.

The street filled with people as Fossett's residents came out of hiding, anxious to see the results of the plan that Walt and Bryce had cooked up during a frantic phone call less than two hours before. As Colton sat handcuffed in the back of a cruiser, the sheriff walked over to find out what had happened. It took fifteen minutes and three people — Bryce, Walt, and Melanie — to explain, but not one of them could answer the biggest question of all.

"Who," the sheriff asked, "shot Colton?"

Heads shook and shoulders were raised in consternation. No one could figure out where the bullet that had taken away both the gun and half of Colton's hand had come from. A second deputy walked over, carrying the gun in a plastic bag.

"Judging from where he was standing and where the gun landed, I'd say it came from somewhere up there."

All eyes turned in the direction of Lou Tsimiak's house. There on his lookout tower stood the last Luckiamute warrior, his face painted, a pair of eagle feathers tied in his plaited hair, wearing the uniform of a U.S. Marine. He raised a fist and brought it down on his chest.

"Oorah!"

The crowd gasped.

"Who the hell is that?" the sheriff said.

"An Indian warrior," Bryce said.

Melanie nodded. "And one hell of a shot."
Walt merely shook his head and grinned.
"Well, I'll be danged."

EPILOGUE

Melanie flinched as the microphone was thrust in her face. No matter how many of these interviews she did, they never seemed to get any easier. Each one felt like the first: Her palms sweated, her hands shook, and her knees felt like rubber. Nevertheless, when she looked around at the changes in her little town, she knew it was more than worth the effort. Fossett wasn't just surviving; it was thriving.

The reporter with the mic gave her a tight smile, still waiting for an answer.

"You're right," Melanie said at last. "It's been quite a ride. If you'd told me a year and a half ago that Fossett would be doing as well as it is, I wouldn't have believed you."

The woman nodded her perfectly coiffed head.

"You will admit, however, that there have been some bumps along the way."

347

"Of course," Melanie said. "Being called The Craziest Town in America was kind of a shock, at first. We knew some people might laugh, and a few of us even wondered if it hit a little too close to home."

She winked.

"When you look at the results, though, it's hard to argue that it was anything but a boon for us."

"Well, you've certainly made a big splash in a short time. I hear Flora's Crazy-Good Pies just made the list of 'Oprah's Favorite Things.' "

"That's right," Melanie said. "And Flora's not the only one in town whose business is thriving."

All around them, people were hurrying toward the auditorium. They needed to wrap this up quickly and get inside.

"Are there any plans to hold another election?"

Melanie paused. There'd been some talk about holding another election — Rod, especially, was still keen — but most people felt that for the time being, at least, having a dog as their mayor was just fine. One day, of course, Shep would be gone, but he still had plenty of years left. For now, she preferred not to think too much about that.

"I think we'll let Shep finish out his term,

348

first, before making that decision."

"The North Korean press is claiming your dog's election proves that democracy is a failure," the woman said. "What's your response to that?"

Melanie laughed.

"Well, it probably wasn't what the Founding Fathers had in mind, but it was the will of the people."

"So, would you say that Fossett's experiment in democracy is going well?"

"Very well. Ask anyone in town and they'll tell you — Shep's a great mayor."

"Tell me, what does a dog mayor do on an average day?"

"Most days, he's on his dog bed at the coffee shop. He greets people when they come in and poses for pictures when people ask. We also found a stamp pad with non-toxic ink, so he can sign autographs. We have had to ask people not to give him treats, though."

"Hence, the sign: 'Please Don't Feed the Mayor.' "

Melanie nodded. So many people wanted to give her dog a treat that he'd gained almost six pounds in the first few months after his election. Now that his weight had returned to normal, Shep's treats were limited to the ones he got from Walt.

"We understand that he does have a few official duties, though."

"Right. Every other Saturday morning — today being one — Shep conducts city business in the high school auditorium. People can come sit in the bleachers and watch."

The cameraman panned across the crowd of people waiting to see Shep conduct the town's business that day. The biweekly "town hall" was actually closer to an amateur theater production than true governance, but that didn't stop people from coming, and the residents loved playing their parts. Everyone who participated came with their own "grievance" to air in front of the mayor, and Jewell Divine was there to interpret Shep's thoughts for the audience. In addition to being fun to watch, the meetings had even mitigated some of the real problems and concerns that came to light. As Melanie had discovered, just giving folks a chance to be heard — even by a dog — was often enough to solve the problem.

"I hear you've been getting some pretty big crowds."

"We have. In fact, we'd better get in there if you want to see him in action."

"I would, yes," the reporter said. "But before we do, what have you learned in the last eighteen months about Fossett and the folks who live here? Do you think it's hurt or helped that so many people still think of this as a crazy town?"

Melanie frowned thoughtfully. For once, someone had asked her a question she hadn't already been asked and answered a dozen times.

"I learned that trying to change people is a losing strategy. People are the way they are; we don't all have to be the same. I also learned that there are lots of ways to define success. We may not have any corporate headquarters or big manufacturers here, but Fossett has a lot of other things going for it: community spirit, civic pride, a below-average cost of living, and abundant natural beauty. If something's made here, we go out of our way to buy it, sell it, and promote it. Because of that, we now have more artists, musicians, and writers per capita than any other city west of the Mississippi. Creative people are attracted to the offbeat, the quirky, the unusual, and people in Fossett like being appreciated for who and what they are.

"As far as being called crazy goes, I guess that depends on what your definition of crazy is. Is it crazy to have a dog for a mayor? Maybe, but people told us we were crazy to base our economy on tourism and the arts, and we're doing fine."

Melanie glanced over and saw Bryce signal her from the door — Shep was about to call the meeting to order. She nodded and smiled at the woman with the mic.

"It might even be crazy for a woman to marry the same man twice," she said, smiling, "but I think I can live with that."

ACKNOWLEDGMENTS

Many many thanks to everyone at Kensington for working tirelessly on my behalf, and to my stalwart agent, Doug Grad. I couldn't do what I do without you.

AUTHOR'S NOTE

The idea of having a dog mayor is not as far-fetched as it sounds. In fact, not only dogs, but cats and other domestic animals have been mayors of several municipalities around the world. The inspiration for this story, however, was Bosco Ramos, a Labrador retriever/Rottweiler mix who was elected mayor of Sunol, California, in 1981. According to Wikipedia, the British tabloid *Daily Star* called Sunol "the wackiest town in the world" for electing a dog as its mayor, and in 1990, the Chinese newspaper *People's Daily* used Bosco's election as an example of the failings of the American electoral process. Bosco served as mayor of Sunol until his death in 1994. A statue of the plucky pooch was erected in front of the Sunol Post Office in 2008.

ABOUT THE AUTHOR

Sue Pethick is an award-winning short-story writer whose life-long love of animals inspired her to write *Boomer's Bucket List, Pet Friendly,* and *The Dog Who Came for Christmas.* Born in San Diego, California, she now lives with her husband in Vancouver, Washington. Please visit Sue online at www.SuePethick.com.